GODDESS OF THE BROKEN

1

All books by Jamie Dalton are fade to black level spice with no swearing. If you enjoy her books but also enjoy options with bit more spice she publishes those under the pen name JD Magnetra. If you want to check out a current list of books published by Jamie Dalton check out her website www.jamieda lton.net

Other Books By Jamie Dalton

Becoming Banneret (Prequel to Worldwalker and Free on her website)

Worldwalker (Banneret Book 1)

Dragonborn (Banneret Book 2)

The Black-Backed Mirror (Prequel to Throne of Slumber and Free on her website)

Throne of Slumber

The Charming Four

Other Books By JD Magnetra

Dragon Heart (Publishing in Realm of Midnight Oct 2023)

Book Cover by Jamie Dalton

Cover Illustration by Christina Schneider

Interior art, formatting and full wrap by Magnetra's Design

This book was initially published on Kindle Vella as it was written. It has since been edited and had extra scenes added from the version that is on there.

CONTENTS

Land of the Gods

Bodia Empire

Forever means nothing if progression isn't possible
As the mortals evolve so must their gods
A mortal trial, the immortal must try
If they succeed the power is theirs
But if they fail, only Fate can decide

Forever means nothing if progression isn't possible
As the mortals evolve so must their gods
A mortal trial, the immortal must try
If they succeed the power is theirs
But if they fail, only Fate can decide

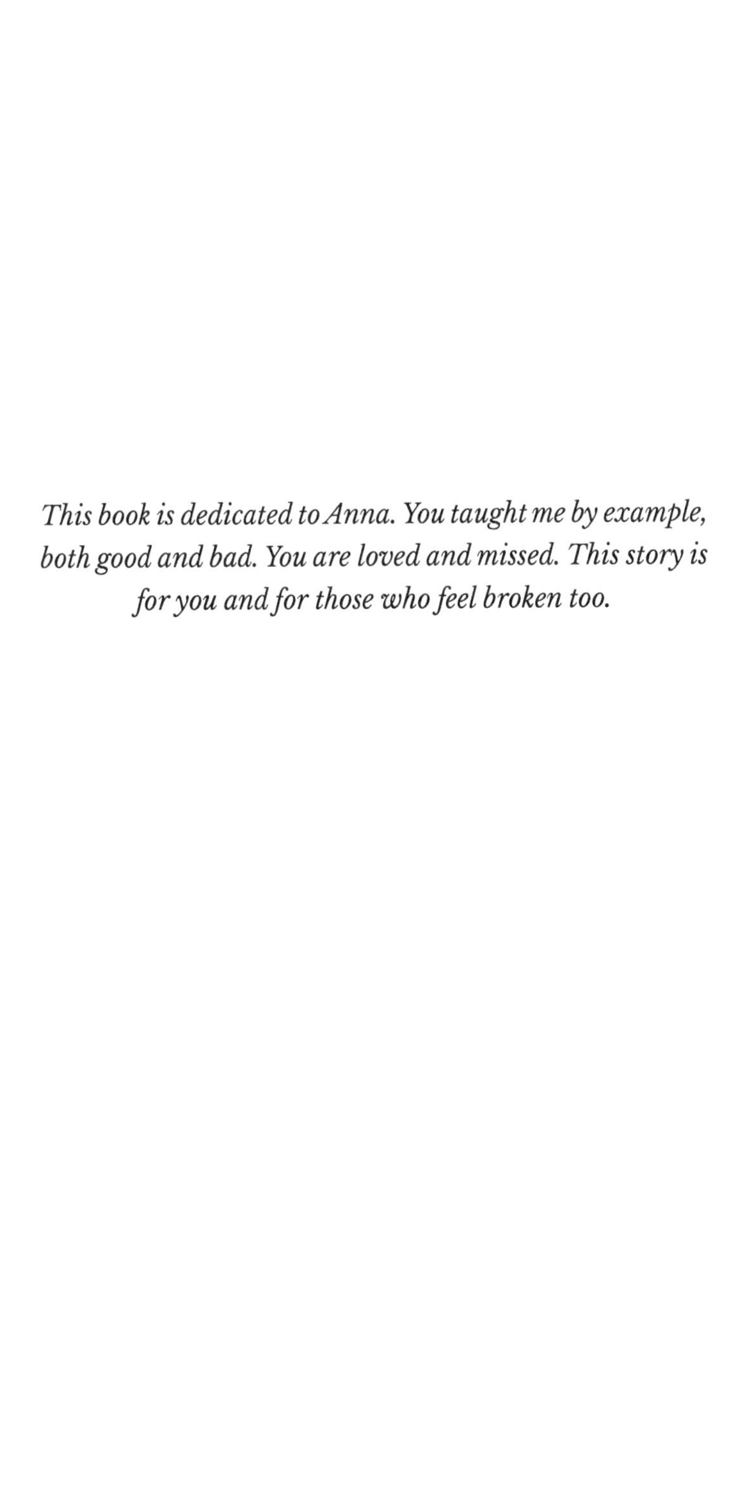

This book is dedicated to Anna. You taught me by example, both good and bad. You are loved and missed. This story is for you and for those who feel broken too.

CHAPTER 1

Tempest knew mortals did three things better than the gods. They loved more fiercely, were quicker to make decisions, and their food was both adventurous and delicious. Something about the shortened life span of mortals drove them to seek perfection in ways that the gods simply overlooked.

After thirteen days of wandering in the desert with no food or water, that third one seemed a step above the others. She had nothing other than the blue linen dress draped across her frame and a few gold coins to get her started in her new life. There was no need for more. Her immortal body didn't require any nourishment and was difficult to harm.

The glaring sun beat down on her pale skin and sand blew through her chestnut brown hair as she made her way through the vast desert between Amna and Brado. Her skin was a glaring reminder of her immortality and the fact that she didn't really belong among mortals. No matter how many years she lived in the desert, it never darkened. She sometimes envied other gods for their brown skin. She'd blend in better among the locals that way.

Tempest held her hand over her eyes and paused to contemplate which direction she would go. It was the way she had lived for hundreds of years. Hiding among the mortals so her gifts couldn't be used by the other gods, and moving every fifteen years so the humans she lived among never discovered that she didn't age as they did. Her ability was helpful in any profession she chose to pursue, and in every city, she decided on a new name and occupation.

She could feel *everything*. Not just material things, but who people really were. It wasn't as though she could read their minds. No; Tempest read their souls and emotions and weighed their righteousness accordingly. That was both her gift and her curse.

For the last hour, a soul had been calling out to her among the sand dunes, a truly broken and wronged soul. It fluttered as if it would soon disappear and journey to Toph, the land of the dead.

She considered ignoring it and continuing on her way. The hope for dandelion shortbread cookies and white tea taunted her taste buds. Something was different about this soul, though. It was almost calling to her specifically, as if it knew her. While she could generally tune out the souls around her with ease, she couldn't shake this one from her consciousness.

The soul wasn't too far out of her way. If she hurried, she could assist the individual and still spend the night in a soft bed.

The connection between her and the soul grew stronger with each step she took towards it. A tightness in her chest grew and worsened the closer she got. Curious and admittedly confused, she quickened her pace. Sensing a soul wasn't unusual; her body reacting to one was.

She climbed to the top of yet another sand dune, her feet constantly sliding in the golden grains beneath her feet. She looked down the other side and saw a man below. Naked, unconscious, and bleeding from multiple wounds, he lay on his side in a haphazard pile of flesh and bones.

Tempest slid down the dune and dropped to her knees beside the man. She didn't touch him at first, assessing how severe his wounds were. Noting the burns covering his body, she swept his long, inky black hair from his chiseled face. It was in better shape than the rest of his body, to her surprise. Almost recognizable, if not for the wounds from whomever had left him here.

Her connection to the soul sent a bolt of searing pain through her chest as his body neared its end. Tempest collapsed in agony onto his body. Her first instinct, to pull herself off to avoid hurting him further, was overridden by a soothing coolness that bled into him from...herself?

She lifted her body off of him but kept one hand tenderly on his side. His wounds were healing. Unbelievable! She didn't have any healing abilities; at least, not in this sense. Her specialty was healing broken hearts. Never before had she healed someone physically. And he had been on the brink of death!

Who is this man? she wondered.

In only moments, his body was entirely healed. Looking over his body in awe, she didn't realize that she was still touching him until tanned and uncalloused fingers gripped her wrist.

Her dark eyes darted up and met a golden pair boring fiercely into hers.

"Who are you, to touch me?" the man demanded.

Too surprised to speak, she only stared back.

His grip tightened. "I said, who are you?"

"Tempest," she sputtered.

It wasn't until after she spoke that she realized her mistake. She'd given him her real name. Whatever Fate desired of her, she needed to take care of it quickly. Tempest couldn't let word of where she was spread before she moved on, or the other gods would find her—something she'd sworn to never let happen.

She ripped her arm from his grip and scooted away as the man sat up. Tempest looked across the sand dunes as his entire body was now revealed, including details she had carefully avoided investigating previously. Grabbing her dress, she tore the bottom third of her skirt off.

"What are you doing?" the man growled.

"Here." She tossed the torn fabric his way. "Cover yourself. I can't guarantee I can heal you again. I'm sure there are some areas you would prefer to not be burned by the sun."

He groaned as he stood.

"I told you who I am. I think it's only fair that you do the same." Tempest tucked a lock of hair behind her ear as a gust of wind blew past them.

"I'm covered. You don't have to avoid looking at me now."

When she turned to look back at him, it almost took her breath away. The sun had dropped just behind him on its way to sleep, creating a crown of light above his head.

The man cleared his throat. "Technically, you gave me a name. You never told me who you were."

She gave her head a shake., "Currently, I'm nobody. I was on my way to Brado for a fresh start when I stumbled upon you."

She squirmed under his unwavering gaze, questioning why he made her nervous. She was a goddess, for crying out loud! There was no reason to feel uneasy about any mortal.

Deciding enough was enough, Tempest rose to her feet and crossed her arms. "Who exactly are you, and why were you dumped out here in the desert to die?"

Silence.

"It's your choice to answer or not, but know that I will leave you here unconscious and lost if you refuse. You will be on your own to find your way back."

His eyes widened. "You would do that?"

Afraid her bluff would be evident if she spoke, she only nodded.

"I don't know by whom, but I assume I was attacked and left for dead because of my position in the kingdom."

"Are you a noble or someone close to the emperor?"

"You could say that."

Tempests raised a brow and shifted to one side. "That wasn't an answer. Who. Are. You?"

He shifted his feet and squared off in a surprisingly imposing stance. "I am Aiden Theopilus, ruler of the Bodian Empire."

Her heart sunk like a heavy stone in an ocean. This was bad. Very, very bad. The only mortals the gods ever thought worthy of their time were nobles and royalty, and they watched them closely. She needed to run.

Afraid her fear would be easily read on her face, Tempest turned and began the slippery climb up a sand dune. She took several deep breaths in an attempt to settle herself, hoping her exertion would shroud the action should he notice it.

"Where are you going?" Aiden demanded.

"I told you," she barked, refusing to look back. "I'm heading to Brado."

"I need to get back to Monstrap. You said you would take me."

She rubbed her chest to ease tightness that became worse with every step.

"Technically, I said I would help you find your way back, not that I would personally take you there. We can reach Brado by nightfall. Find food, drink, and possibly a bed to sleep in. Monstrap is a three-day walk that way." Tempest pointed to her left. "It's your decision which way you go, but I'm going to sleep with a full stomach tonight."

A dusting of sand blew past her on the wind from Aiden's frustrated kick before he began following her. She smirked, knowing she'd won this round.

The clenching in her chest calmed but didn't recede. Curious, she slowed down to allow Aiden to catch up. As she suspected, she felt less tension as the distance between them shortened. Whatever game Fate was playing, it did not make Tempest happy.

"Are you a priestess?" Aiden asked as they reached the top of the dune.

"No." She shot him a look, raising her brow. "Why would you think that?"

"You healed me. Not just treated my wounds, but actually healed me. That's something only those blessed by the gods can do."

She snorted. "Trust me, the gods wouldn't choose me to bestow their gifts upon. Eshum prefers more humble and obedient followers to carry out his work."

"Not a fan of the god of health, I take it?"

"You could say that."

Tempest reached out and caught Aiden as his legs gave out under him, preventing him from tumbling down the side of the dune. Pulling him back to his feet, she held onto his arm until he was steady.

"You've got to be more careful. I basically just pulled you back from the gates of Toph. I doubt I could heal you again if you broke your neck because you pushed yourself too hard, too fast."

Aiden yanked his harm from her grip. "Got it. Wouldn't want you to exert yourself."

She sighed as he continued walking. "It's not that I wouldn't try to. I genuinely don't know if I could. I've never done that before."

She received only a grunt in return. The two walked in uncomfortable silence as the sun slowly sank below the horizon. The appearance of Brado was a welcome sight as the last rays of the golden sun disappeared and the stars began their display.

Aiden shivered.

"Are you alright?" Tempest asked.

His words stuttered from between chattering teeth. "F-f-f-fine. Jus-s-st getting c-c-c-c-cold."

While the temperature had dropped with the sun, it wasn't cold enough yet to cause someone to shiver to this degree. Concerned, she placed a hand on his forehead.

"You have a fever." She cursed herself for not noticing sooner. "You've pushed your body too hard for what it has gone through. Here, let me help you."

Tempest moved to support him only to be shoved away.

"I said I'm f-f-f-fine."

Shoulders slumped, Aiden pushed himself forward. Tempest followed close behind, catching him when he stumbled. While frustrated that he refused her help otherwise , she couldn't help but be impressed at the resilience of this mortal. Especially when one took into consideration the pampered life he led.

It took three tries to find an inn that would take them. The first was full, while the second took one look at Aiden's sickly disposition and refused. Their last option charged double for a small room in what Tempest guessed was a small storage shed behind the actual inn.

Aiden collapsed on a cot in the corner of the small adobe building. It was small and roughly circular in shape, its interior only lit by rays of light that peeked through the slits in the door. He immediately fell asleep. His breathing slowed, and his chest barely rose with each breath.

Grabbing a blanket from one of the piles in the room, Tempest draped it over him and quietly left in search of food. She ignored the tightening of her chest as she left him and entered the inn only a few feet away.

"Is your friend alright?" a large woman asked as she brushed crumbs from the apron covering her red dress.

"He will be. He was in the desert too long and needs food and water to regain his strength."

The woman nodded. "Ah, that's why he looked so bad. The desert can defeat the best of us."

Something about the woman called to Tempest's ability, but as she was already taking care of one mortal, she chose to ignore it. She followed the woman towards a counter, where a bowl of crusty bread, a bottle of herbed oil, and a jug of water were soon placed in front of her.

"Have you ever had a prickly pear?" the woman asked.

"It's been a long time, but yes."

Wrinkles appeared at the corner of her eyes as a warm smile spread across the woman's face. "My sister's husband grows them. They're the sweetest you'll find around here. Would you care for some?"

Tempest's mouth watered at the thought of it. Setting three copper coins on the counter, she asked, "Would this be enough to cover it?"

The woman smiled. "The two of you look like you've had a rough go of it." She grabbed two of the coins and tucked them in a hidden pocket of her dress. "Keep the other for another meal. The name's Tavora. If you need me, you know where to find me."

For the first time in what felt like forever, Tempest smiled. "Thank you."

She loaded her arms with the food and headed back. She started to run as cries rang out from the small building where she'd left Aiden. The door slammed open as she entered, ready for a fight.

Aiden whimpered in his sleep and cried out again. She set everything down on the floor and closed the door before approaching his tossing form and reaching out.

As soon as she touched him, his hand gripped her throat. She pried his fingers far enough off her windpipe that she could breathe, but he didn't release her completely.

"Aiden," she squeaked.

His eyes opened but didn't focus.

Tempest tried again. "Aiden, it's me."

His eyes locked with hers, but the person she'd found in the desert wasn't there. The man looking at her now was ancient, deadly, and vulnerable.

"I found you, Tempest. It's been so long."

Chapter 2

Tempest froze.

Gods occasionally came down in mortal form as a test to increase their power. They had to endure a list of trials before they could advance while having no recollection of who they were before the trial. Apparently, the life of a blessed god wasn't difficult enough to foster growth otherwise.

Aiden leaned forward, his voice neither threatening nor reassuring. "Where have you been hiding?"

It had been several hundred years since she'd encountered another god. While she remembered them all clearly, their voices and appearances were a bit hazy in her mind.

She slapped him across the cheek. His head snapped to the side.

Aiden's hand flew to his face, and he slowly turned back in her direction. "What was that for?!"

Tempest searched his eyes, but found no sign of the god she had just been speaking with. The god's consciousness was gone, and Emperor Aiden had returned.

She turned to avoid his gaze and picked up the water. "You were sleep talking. Nonsense that I couldn't understand. I woke you up." She shrugged and held the water out towards him. "Would you like a drink?"

He skeptically accepted the water and began to drink. He handed the jug back to her, and her heart sank a little when she realized it was empty.

"Did you not already have some?"

She shook her head. "It's fine. I can get more later. There's food for you as well. Feel free to eat."

Picking up a prickly pear, she moved away and settled on a pile of blankets.

"Why didn't you say anything? You must have been in the desert at least as long as I was. I saw no water pouch. It absolutely is not fine. Let me get..."

Aiden attempted to stand, only to collapse on the floor instead. Tempest rushed to help him back up.

"You fool. You were practically dead only a few hours ago. You need to recover. I can get more."

He glared at her as she helped him back onto the cot. "You think it acceptable to call your emperor a fool?"

"If that's how you choose to behave, then yes, I do."

She picked up the bread and oil and set them on the bed beside him. "Eat. You need to regain your strength if you're going to make it back to your palace."

He watched her settle back onto the blankets and broke off a piece of bread. "What do you mean by *you*? You're accompanying me."

She scoffed. "I never said such a thing. You've made it to town and are safe. Hire someone to take you."

"With what money?" Aiden gestured towards the strip of fabric around his waist. "It's not like I have pockets full of gold."

She rolled her eyes. "I'm sure once it's discovered that you are the beloved emperor, someone will help you. Maybe they'll give you a line of credit until you make it home and are able to pay them."

The bread in Aiden's hand crumbled. "I should have you beheaded."

Tempest chuckled. "I would love to see you try," she muttered under her breath.

"What was that?" Aiden put his hand on the edge of the cot and attempted to rise again.

Waving her hands in front of her, she replied, "Nothing. Just eat your food. Tomorrow we'll find you some clothes and figure out how to get you home."

Their eyes locked in an unspoken standoff. Aiden tore another piece of bread, dipped it in the herbed oil, and ate it without looking away.

Rolling her eyes again, Tempest turned and leaned against the wall. She pulled a blanket over herself and closed her eyes. Soon this man would be someone else's problem, and she would find another town to go to, somewhere she couldn't be traced to by him. At least, if Fate would allow it.

Tempest was awoken by a sharp pain in her chest. The room was empty; Emperor Aiden had disappeared. Using the pain as a compass, she left the inn's grounds and walked up the stone street to find him.

Getting the emperor back to his palace may not be as easy as she'd assumed. In the daylight, the patched cracks on the sandstone buildings showed the wear and tear of the town. This was not a wealthy area. Obtaining credit with only the promise of later payment would be difficult.

Soon the sounds of a crowd reached her ears. As she approached, a small market opened up. Stalls with a rainbow of colored fabric covers lined the street. The energy of the crowd both energized and put Tempest on edge.

A woman readjusted bolts of cloth to better show the colors in a stall under an emerald-green roof. She grunted at a few customers and hollered in a different direction. A man with a spice stall picked up a jar of bright yellow powder that rolled away, shaking it to ensure it was still full. A small child bumped into Tempest's leg, their mother quickly apologizing as she hustled them away.

Swaying on her feet, Tempest tested which way to go to find the emperor. Noting a slight easing of the pain when she leaned towards the left, she continued that way. Her stomach rumbled at the smell of loomi tea as she passed a stall with a bright blue fabric top.

Stalls of dates, chickens, clay pottery, and fabrics lined the street. Their owners called after her, encouraging her to stop and investigate their wares. Amid the crowd, Tempest almost missed the feeling in her chest getting worse again. Backtracking, she eyed a small alley. The feeling eased as she tested a few steps towards it, confirming the direction she needed to go.

She heard scuffling feet ahead. As she approached another alley that intersected the one she was in, a group of half a dozen men gathered around something came into view. She was tempted to avoid them, but the pull in her chest told her she needed to head toward them. Keeping her footsteps completely silent, Tempest slowly approached the tight grouping of men and peeked through a gap between them.

A body lay on the ground. As one of the men shifted to kick the lifeless person, she caught a better view of their target. The tattered blue fabric matched her dress.

Rage overcame her, and with a yell, she summoned Soulshadow, a ball with four sharp hooks attached to a chain that grew and shrunk at her will. Allowing the chain to wrap around her body as she spun, Tempest swung the ball towards the nearest man. The hooks gripped into his shoulder, and with a hard yank, he flew past her, dropping to the ground after colliding with the hard stone wall.

Fate had led Tempest to the emperor, and Tempest knew better than to let it down. Rarely did that go well for anyone, mortal or god.

Chapter 3

With a flick of her wrist, Soulshadow answered Tempest's call and returned to her hand. The chain slipped through her fingers a short way as she began to spin the ball again.

A man in orange robes charged toward her. She let Soulshadow lose, allowing a small chuckle to slip through her lips at the sound of his skull cracking.

Soulshadow returned to her hand once again. The four remaining men approached her cautiously. Ball spinning, she circled around the wall of a two-story building, preventing them from surrounding her.

All four men charged at the same time. Crouching low, Tempest leaned back, allowing one of them to hurdle over her. Soulshadow flew around his waist, and when she yanked, he flew back over her and collided with one of the other men. She spun and kicked her leg out, knocking both standing men to the ground.

Tempest rose. Soulshadow slammed into the jaw of the one who'd been leveled by the hurdler as she reclaimed her weapon from his waist.

The two remaining men had risen but now froze. She took a single step towards them, and both took off running down the alley. Though she was tempted to chase after them, Tempest glanced toward Aiden. With blood running from his mouth and nose, she chose him instead.

Soulshadow's chain and ball disappeared when Tempest crouched down. Sliding her arms under Aiden's knees and back, she lifted him into her arms and returned to the inn they had stayed in the night before.

No words were needed, and the innkeeper only nodded in understanding and pointed to the building they had stayed in before. Tempest entered and laid Aiden down on the cot.

Moments later, Tavora quietly entered with clean water, cloths, and a jar of salve.

"Looks like the two of you have had a rough go of it again. Thought you may need these."

Tempest smiled at the woman. "Thank you."

Dipping the cloth into the water, she began to clean the blood from Aiden's face.

The woman watched, fidgeting with her fingers. "You know, I've never met a woman like you."

"Oh, is that so?"

"You just carried a full-grown man as if he were a child."

Tempest hesitated. "I've had weapons training since I was very young. It's quite common where I'm from for women to be stronger than they appear."

The woman nodded. "If you say so. Is there anything I can do for you, dear?"

"No, thank you. I appreciate you letting us stay here again." Tempest brushed a lock of hair from Aiden's face as she cleaned the blood from his nose. "I'm not sure how long he will need to recover."

"Don't worry about that. You can stay as long as you need."

"We would appreciate your discretion about us being here," Tempest said, turning to look at Tavora. "We wouldn't want any trouble to follow us back."

"Of course. I'll leave you to it. Come over when you're ready and grab something to feed him when he wakes up."

"I will. Thank you."

Tempest turned back to Aiden as the woman left.

After wiping the rest of the blood from his face, she began dabbing salve onto his wounds. Aiden groaned, then slowly opened his eyes.

Tempest pulled her hand back. "Welcome back, Emperor Aiden."

He quickly turned towards her, then flinched and let out another groan. "Why did I just do that?"

"Are you all right?"

Aiden stared at her in silence for a moment. "Who are you?"

Tempest sighed. “I thought we already went over this.” She pointed towards her chest. “Tem-pest. Just how hard did they hit you?”

“I saw... you. Vaguely.” His brows furrowed.

“Do you see me now, solidly?”

Another groan cut off his laugh as it became painful. “You saved me. I saw you...fight them. Defeat them.”

Tempest rose and sat on the pile of blankets. She watched him for a moment, contemplating how much of the truth she should reveal.

“Yes, I did.”

Aiden rolled on his side so he could see her better. “You are unlike any woman I’ve ever met.”

She shrugged. “So I’ve been told.”

“Did you carry me here as well, or was that just a dream?”

She leaned forward with an elbow on her knee and smirked. “What do you think?”

He groaned again as he rolled onto his back. “I think you should have healed me again.”

“I told you, that was my first time. I also remember saying you should be careful because I didn’t know if it was possible to do it again.”

Aiden didn’t reply.

Tempest broke the silence, pointing at the bowl of salve. “You should put some of that on your bruises. You were beat up pretty bad.”

He sighed and looked towards the wall. “I’m not sure I can. It hurts too much to move.”

"If you ask nicely, I am willing to help."

"Emperors do not ask things of their citizens."

"They do if they want *this* citizen to help them."

He mumbled a few words, too quiet to hear.

"What was that?"

He paused a moment before answering, "I said, will you help me?"

"Don't forget to say please."

He turned his head towards her. "Please."

Tempest rose and moved to sit on the edge of the cot, ignoring the venom that practically dripped from that single word. "See, that wasn't so hard. People are much more willing to help you if you ask nicely. They'll usually do a better job of it, too, if they do it of their own free will. A little ruler-of-all-the-lands tip for you."

He groaned as she rubbed salve on a bruise forming on his shoulder. "Who are you to give me advice?"

"Nobody special. Just someone who has saved your life twice in less than a day. Possibly the only person you can currently trust, at least until you figure out who tried to murder you."

Aiden watched as she dipped her fingers in the bowl and prepared to rub salve across his stomach. "Thank you," he said softly.

Tempest paused and allowed a smile to spread across her face and reach her eyes. "You're welcome."

He flinched as she continued to work the salve into his skin. "You're right. I don't know who I can trust."

"What do you plan to do about that?"

Aiden's hand slowly moved to rest atop hers. As if the words themselves were painful, he asked, "Would you be willing to help me?"

She laughed. "After asking so nicely, how can I refuse?"

His brow furrowed. "Are you making fun of me?" he growled.

"I would never, your majesty," she responded lightly, not bothering to hide the glint in her eye. "As soon as you are healed enough, we will find transportation and get you back to your castle. I'll help you figure out who tried to kill you."

His hand moved away from hers as he closed his eyes and nodded.

Chapter 4

Tempest entered the inn with a tray of empty cups and bowls. She carried her goods to the sink and placed them in it herself. The dining room was full, and the counter was likewise without an open seat. Tempest looked for Tavora and was unsuccessful, but did find a younger woman bussing another table and approached her.

"Do you need any help?"

The woman handed a pile of plates over and picked up the mugs on the table. "Thank you! I didn't expect to see you in here during our rush. Of course this would be when they come to talk to Tavora!"

"Honestly, I've lost track of the time and didn't realize it would be," Tempest said, following her into the kitchen. "Is everything all right? Do you need me to stay and help you?"

The woman glanced at the door with a look of concern and replied, "No, dear, you're a guest. I couldn't do that to you." She deposited the mugs she was carrying into the sink and wiped her hands on her apron. "I appreciate the help you've already given, though. The clothes you ordered are in and by the back door."

"Thank you."

"I assume you'll be leaving soon?"

"My companion decided he has healed enough and is eager to be on our way," Tempest answered with a nod. "He could really use a few more days, but I understand he is anxious to return home. I appreciate your help in gathering the supplies we need and arranging transportation. We'll leave first thing in the morning."

The woman placed her hand on Tempest's arm and smiled. "I'm glad I could help. I best be getting back to my customers."

Tempest watched the woman greet her next customer and moved to the back door. She picked up the packages waiting for her and exited with one last glance around the bustling room.

As Tempest made her way back to Aiden, she felt a sudden sense of unease, as if something was wrong or someone was in danger. She quickened her pace and turned the corner, discovering Tavora surrounded by three men. One of them had grabbed her arm, and she looked to be in distress. Tempest didn't hesitate to intervene.

"Let her go!"

The man holding Tavora tightened his grip and sneered at Tempest. "This doesn't concern you, woman."

"Like Toph it doesn't!" Tempest answered. She could feel Tavora's soul crying out for help, and she wasn't about to stand by and do nothing.

"Tempest, please, just go!" Tavora pleaded, her voice shaking with fear.

"I'm not going anywhere," Tempest said firmly. She turned her attention back to the men, her glare icy with anger. "You have exactly one minute to release her, or I will make you regret every moment of your miserable lives."

One man stepped towards Tempest. "Unless you are taking on her debt yourself, this does not concern you. Though I'm sure we could find a use for a woman such as yourself."

Tempest felt sick. It took every effort to not feel dirty from the darkness of these men's souls. "I'm warning you; let her go, *now*."

The man smiled. "I think you're bluffing."

The other men approached, moving as one toward her. The man holding Tavora's arm released her to do so. Tempest took a step back, her eyes never losing sight of any of them. Her senses were alert and ready; she had no intention of letting them harm anyone.

"How much does she owe?"

The men continued to slowly walk towards her. "More than you could possibly have," the man who'd been holding Tavora sneered.

"That's not an answer." Tempest pulled a small handful of gold coins from her pocket and held them out in front of her. "Is this enough?"

"Is that all you have?"

A glance at Tavora's wide eyes told Tempest that it was more than enough. "Take it and leave her be. I want it in writing that her debt is cleared."

The men laughed as they closed in on her. "What's it to you?"

Her patience completely gone, Tempest reached out and brushed against their souls with her own. It was a warning she hoped would be enough to prevent them from turning violent. Their faces paled.

One reached out and snatched the gold before stepping back. "It's enough."

"Good. Go inside and write out the receipt. I expect proof before you leave, or I will come find you myself."

The men hurried inside and Tavora stumbled over to Tempest, grabbing onto the skirt of Tempest's dress as her legs gave out under her, accidentally knocking the packages from Tempest's hands. She reached down to help Tavora up.

"Are you all right?"

"That... that was a small fortune you just gave them."

"To some. Let me know if they don't leave the receipt for you."

Tavora bent down to pick up the pile of clothing and brushed it off as she handed it back. "I take it this means you are leaving soon."

"It does. I wanted to thank you before leaving. Your kindness will not be forgotten."

"Oh, no dear, the favor you have just done me is much more than anything I did for you. I will never be able to repay your kindness."

Tempest could feel the elation of the woman's soul. It felt free and unencumbered, the opposite of how it had the entire time she had known her. "Let us call it even. I wish you the best."

"And I, you." Tavora smiled and waved as she made her way back into the tavern.

Her heart lightened, Tempest turned to prepare her traveling companion for their long journey ahead.

Aiden groaned as he slid off the camel. His knees buckled as his feet sank into the soft sand. Tempest approached with a jug of water and offered it to him.

"Who knew that you would lack the gracefulness one would expect from your station. Thirsty?"

He glared up at her. Rising to his feet and dusting his new white robes off, he replied, "Why don't you try riding one of these all day and see how gracefully you dismount the beast?"

She laughed and shook her head. "I learned that lesson, once. Never again. Unless you ride them frequently, you will be sore for days in areas you never knew existed."

Aiden took a swig of water and handed the jug back to her. "You could have warned me."

She shrugged. "What fun would that have been? It does tell me how rarely you leave your palace, though."

"Oh? How so?"

"If you traveled much, you would have already experienced the discomfort of riding. Perhaps even decided not to insist on us paying for an extra camel. You do know that you will be reimbursing me for all of this, correct?"

He only nodded.

Their guide called for the two of them to join the rest of the group and assist in setting up camp for the night. Tempest waved a hand, signaling for Aiden to go first, and chuckled to herself as he waddled over to the rest of the caravan. Several families with children stood around the leader and followed his men to help set up camp. Tempest and Aiden assisted with unloading the camels and were soon on their bedrolls by a fire.

Tempest laid back and admired the stars as they began to appear in the dusk sky. "So, what's our story?"

Aiden lowered onto his side and propped his head up with his arm. "For what?"

"For me joining you. You can't expect me to just walk into your palace with you and not seem suspicious. Whoever did this to you will become wary of me immediately."

"I didn't think of that." Aiden looked towards the fire in contemplation. "What if you were there as a representative for Dei Electi?"

Her head whipped in his direction. "Excuse me!? You can't be serious!"

"Why not?"

"You truly expect me to join the competition to become empress? You do realize that the gods and goddesses choose their own representatives; it would anger them to take that away from them."

Dei Electi had been a favorite entertainment for the gods for centuries. Before leaving the land of the gods, Tempest had enjoyed it, as well, finding a woman she thought would best represent herself and serve the people and then sponsoring her in the contest. Each woman would be blessed by whatever god chose her, and if she was selected, the kingdom would be blessed by that god.

What Tempest did not appreciate was that occasionally the gods would abandon their mortal if they weren't chosen, and she was left to clean up the mess.

Aiden looked into Tempest's eyes. "Not all of the gods have chosen representatives yet. It's been several hundred years since they have. The goddess of the broken has the right to choose someone and hasn't. You do share her name, and after saving me not once, but twice, I could see her potentially choosing you, anyway, if she were to participate. Honestly, she probably won't even notice."

"She'll know."

"Oh? How are you so sure?"

"I just... know."

He smirked. "How do you know that she will care or disapprove?"

Tempest's mind raced to try to think of another reason, any other reason, for being in Aiden's court without tipping off his enemy. Unable to develop an alternative, she sighed and looked back at the night sky. "Fine."

A smile spread across Aiden's face. "Thank you."

"You owe me."

"I already owe you my life. What more could you possibly want?"

She didn't answer. This wouldn't be easy. There was no way the other gods wouldn't recognize her. She would be targeted constantly. In order to survive, she needed a plan.

Chapter 5

While entering the walls of Monstrap should have put Tempest at ease, it felt as if she were on her way to a chopping block. She was not pleased. She had avoided the gaze of other gods for centuries, and suddenly it seemed as if Fate was forcing her to enter that world once again.

She raised a hand to block the sun and looked up at Aiden atop his camel. She'd bartered with a family in the caravan for a keffiyeh, or headcloth, to protect Aiden's identity and his already blistering skin. Without knowing who had attempted to assassinate him, she needed to protect him to the best of her ability. While he would have a layer of protection within his castle walls, in the middle of the capital's bustling streets, she feared he would be an easy target if recognized.

Their party slowly made their way deeper into the whitewashed sandstone city. Homes grew more prominent the further they went. The worn stones of the street felt jarring to her knees after walking on the sand for so long. Individuals and families departed from the caravan one at a time towards their own destinations until all that was left was the two of them.

Tempest kept alert, watching the crowd and edges of the homes and alleys for not only movement, but potentially souls with ill intent. The emotions of the crowd almost overwhelmed her. Her fingers grazed the fabric of her dress in circles as she attempted to ground herself and pick out only those who may be a real threat.

She couldn't help feeling Aiden's anxious and worried soul beside her. She lifted her hand rose and rested it on his calf. He looked down at her from his seat atop the camel, eyes wide with surprise. Tempest gave him a reassuring smile and slight nod before removing her hand.

Something nagged at her. She had found Aiden left for dead in the middle of the desert. If the emperor was known to be dead, the city would show signs of mourning. Tempest could see how the word may not have spread yet to the other cities, but the capital and castle would surely have known. How were they keeping this a secret?

Soon the castle gates loomed over them, only shadowed by the castle that the walls contained. The castle was a deep but subtle shade of grey, as if the sand from the desert had been mixed into the mortar and stone blocks. It was a stark and threatening contrast compared to the white of the city. The castle stood at least three stories high, and its towers reached for the sky. Anchored in the center of the castle, the emperor's keep stood tall, its spires and arches reaching for the heavens.

Two guards stepped forward and blocked their way at the gate. "Halt! The emperor is not seeing civilians today. No entrance allowed."

Aiden slid off his camel, landing a little more gracefully than he had the day before. Standing tall, he asked, "Why are the gates closed?"

"Are you deaf?" one of the guards said with a smirk. "We said no admittance today—for anyone."

Tempest could feel confidence rolling off the guards in waves.

Aiden stepped towards them. "I can understand why the emperor is not seeing anyone today, but you *will* let me in."

"Oh? *Do* you understand? What, exactly, do you understand?"

Unsure if the anger she was feeling was her own or Aiden's, Tempest stepped between him and the guard, whose fist clenched. "Do you not recognize your own emperor in front of you?"

A single chuckle escaped the guard's lips as he approached Tempest, not stopping until his nose almost touched hers. The smell of ale wafted into her nose as he spat out, "I do not, and never will, answer to a woman. Step aside before I throw both of you in the stocks."

Aiden put a hand on Tempest's shoulder and tried to pull her back, but she stood firm. She allowed a bit of her godly power to trickle into her voice as she retorted, "I suggest you open the gates before I do it for you. I am Tempest, representative for the goddess of the broken in the right of Dei Electi. You will feel her wrath if you do not let us enter."

The effect of her words was immediately apparent. Both guards hurried back to their posts, eyes wide, and called for the gates to be opened.

Aiden put the camel's reins in Tempest's hand. "I can't enter leading my own beast. We need to get in and find someone who will recognize me."

She took a deep breath to calm her anger. "Understood."

"You know, you're sort of terrifying."

At that, she smiled. "I know."

As soon as the gates groaned to a halt, they entered an almost empty courtyard. Tempest could feel the eyes of the guards patrolling the walls on her, but she refused to look their way. If they were going to make it through this alive, she needed to show no fear.

A slender man in bright red robes hurried towards them with several servants following close behind. He brushed crumbs from his scraggly beard as he stopped in front of Tempest.

"You are here for Dei Electi? Who do you represent?"

Confused as to why he ignored Aiden, she quickly answered, "Tempest, goddess of the broken."

His eyes widened with surprise. "It has been a very long time since she has submitted a contestant. Do you have her token?"

She had forgotten about this. A token was always given by a god to their chosen to prove that they were a legitimate representative. She groaned internally, knowing she would need to make up an excuse for Aiden later as to how she had one.

Tempest slid her hand through a slit in her dress to access her pocket as she called her token to hand. She presented it to the man with a smile. "Do you mean this?"

His hand shook as he slowly moved a finger across the large gold coin in her palm. He traced the path of Soulshadow's chains as they wove across the surface and stopped on the ball. He read the words etched around the edge in a whisper. "Revenge does not heal the soul. Only forgiveness can truly give eternal peace."

He slowly looked from the coin to her face.

"Does this suffice?" she asked.

He nodded and removed his hand, straightening as he did so. "It does. It's curious that the goddess of the broken has decided to participate in this generation when she has not deemed it necessary to do so for so long."

Tucking the coin into her pocket, Tempest shrugged. "I am not privy to the inner workings of the goddess's mind. I am only here to represent her."

"Yes, yes, of course. If you and your party would follow me—"

"How is it possible that one of my own inner court does not recognize his emperor when he stands before him?" Aiden interrupted.

The man froze. His head jerked to Aiden, and he immediately dropped to his knees, head bowed and hands on the ground. "Forgive me, Emperor Aiden! I was summoned for the representative and hadn't taken in her party yet."

Aiden glared down at the man with arms crossed. "That is no excuse, Sir Eb. I have been gone for several days, yet all seems to be in order."

"W-w-we were told y-you were sick," Sir Eb said, trembling. "R-r-r-resting before the d-d-Dei Electi started."

"Do I look like I've been resting?"

"N-n-n-no, your m-m-majesty!"

"Have someone take this beast and deal with the guards at the gate for not recognizing their ruler. I expect the court to be in the main chamber in one hour and explanations to be made."

Tempest handed the camel's rope to a servant and followed closely behind Aiden as he strode up the palace's steps. The rage emanating from him was palpable, but something else bubbled under the surface, which intrigued her—there was a calm under the storm. It made her very glad his anger was not directed at her.

Chapter 6

For the first time ever, Tempest wished she had brought some of her personal items from her previous life with her. She had expected her most recent move to be a typical one; change her name, her occupation, and start over completely fresh, with no strings or traces of her old life to make it easy to find her.

Now she sat in a massive bedroom, nursing an ache in her chest, with nothing to change into. She used her fingers to comb the knots from her hair. Sand and dust shook from her clothes and hair onto the indigo rug. It had been too long to remember since Tempest last sat on such a soft bed. A soft sigh escaped her lips as she finished with her hair and laid back on the white and blue mound of plush pillows and blankets.

She had been escorted to a wing near the royal one, built generations ago for the contestants of Dei Electi. Tempest hadn't seen any of the other eleven contestants on her way to her room, but she also wasn't sure how many of them were already there.

Then again, she hadn't even known Dei Electi had been called until Aiden told her.

She'd spent the last hour exploring the room. Two tall shelves of books sat on either side of a fireplace. Tempest couldn't imagine it got much use, but the nights did tend to get cold. A long blue couch sat in front of it with small round wooden tables on either end, which were painted with highly detailed white flowers and lines. A pair of tall-backed chairs sat near double doors that opened up onto a courtyard with a tiled fountain and lush greenery. She noted the four other sets of doors that shared the courtyard with her.

Every bit of the room was clearly designed to show the wealth and status of the emperor's household. The attached bathroom was no exception. It had been so long since Tempest had more than a chamber pot and washbasin—truly, not since she left the land of the gods. The deep, tiled bath with hot and cold water faucets, gold-leafed ornate mirror, and white stone sink set in a carved wooden cabinet were more elaborate than the ones she'd had in the land of the gods.

Tempest sat up on the bed at a light knock on the door. "Come in."

A willowy woman in simple red clothes entered, with two guards carrying a large trunk in tow. "His Majesty asked me to supply you with a few items to hold you over until you can acquire your own clothing."

"Thank you." Tempest rose and brushed off the skirt of her dress. "I greatly appreciate a change of clothes."

The woman's eyes widened at the sight of Tempest's bare feet and ankles and motioned for the men to place the trunk near the wardrobe.

"I brought everything you should need." She watched the men exit and moved to open the trunk before continuing, "Do you wish to bathe before getting dressed?"

Tempest inhaled as the smell of jasmine hit her nose when the woman opened a box of soaps and glass bottles. "That would be lovely. Thank you."

The woman smiled. "Of course! I can't imagine you've had many opportunities to use running water indoors. Follow me, and I will show you how everything works in the bathroom. I will set everything up out here and bring you a change of clothes when I've unpacked for you."

Tempest followed the woman into the bathroom and listened to her instruction.

"Do you need anything before I go unpack?" the woman eventually asked.

"I don't think so. Thank you..."

"Sylvia. My name is Sylvia."

"Thank you, Sylvia."

"It's my pleasure. I will just be out here if you need me."

Sylvia exited, closing the bathroom door behind her.

Tempest turned towards the now filling tub and poured out a small portion of the heavenly smelling liquid from the bottle before undressing and slipping in. She sighed as she allowed the water to cover her body. The tension in her muscles began to ease immediately. She let her mind relax and drift away until she was almost asleep.

Her chest tightened, wrenching Tempest back to the present. Rubbing her hand over her heart, she tried to feel if Aiden was moving further away or coming closer. She assumed his meeting with his ministers must be over. She hadn't felt him move for quite a while.

The tightness slowly eased, confirming that he was coming closer. She quickly washed and excited the tub, wrapping herself in a large white towel. While he could be heading anywhere, the last thing she wanted was to be in a state of undress if he came to check on her.

Exiting the bathroom, she found Sylvia straightening the pillows on the bed.

"You're already finished?" Sylvia said, somewhat surprised.

"I loved every minute of it, but wanted to get dressed in case I have any visitors. Do you mind emptying the tub for me while I dress?"

"Are you sure you don't need any assistance?"

Tempest offered her warmest smile as she sensed Aiden moving closer. "I should be fine. I will let you know if I need any help."

"Of course. I will be out once I've cleaned up."

Tempest watched the woman enter the bathroom and turned her attention towards the wardrobe. Two drawers filled with the softest undergarments she had ever felt were at the bottom. She could only hope the dresses were just as comfortable. She was not disappointed when she opened the doors and a wide array of colors greeted her.

Grabbing an emerald gown, she slipped it over her undergarments, the fabric sliding easily across her freshly oiled skin. Glancing around as she closed the doors, she spotted a jade comb on the nightstand. She snatched it up and began working the knots from her hair.

She felt him getting closer with each passing moment. Either their quarters were very close, or the emperor was on his way to see her.

The tightness disappeared, and she could finally take a deep breath again. Twisting her hair into a quick knot at her neck and securing it with a pin, she rose and moved towards the door. Someone knocked just as she came within reach. It had to be him.

Tempest opened the door, revealing Aiden and several guards on the other side.

She offered a small curtsy. "Your majesty."

Aiden's face lit up as he took in her appearance. "I see you're settling in well."

She smiled in return. "I am, thanks to you."

"Do you mind if I come in? I would like to talk for a moment."

Tempest held her arm out in welcome, stepping to the side. "Of course. Please..."

There was a loud crash behind her, and both she and Emperor Aiden jumped as his guards into rush the room.

Chapter 7

Tempest moved to block Aiden from whatever caused the sound with her body, ready to call Soulshadow if needed. Her eyes quickly found Sylvia on her knees, head to the floor, hunched over broken glass. The guards surrounded her as the scent of jasmine hit Tempest's nose once again.

Seeing that there was no danger, Tempest moved to help Sylvia.

"Your Majesty! I'm so sorry," Sylvia blubbered. Her fingers trembled as she began picking up the broken shards. Tempest dropped to her knees and grabbed Sylvia's hands just as a shard sliced the tip of her finger.

"Be careful. Here," Tempest led Sylvia to one of the chairs and handed her a cloth from the trunk. "Let me clean this up. The calluses on my fingers make them tough to cut."

Tempest dropped to her knees and began gathering the pieces in a second cloth she'd removed from the trunk. Careful not to look up, she nevertheless kept an eye on Sylvia and Aiden as she worked.

He watched her with interest, hands at his side and oblivious to his guards who had rejoined him.

She lifted a large piece of the broken glass and dropped it again with a gasp.

Aiden stepped towards her. "Are you all right? Did you injure yourself, as well?"

With a hand raised to stop him from coming closer, she replied, "I'm fine."

Lifting the glass again, she pulled a golden star nestled within a crescent moon out from under it. A delicate gold chain dangled through her fingers as she investigated her find.

"I was bringing it to you," Sylvia blurted out. "I thought you must have left it in the bathroom and didn't want it to get lost. I wasn't keeping it, I swear!"

A pang of pain hit Tempest's heart as Sylvia spoke. She couldn't dig deeper right now, as there were too many people around, but her ability was calling to her. She would need to help this woman's heart heal before she would find peace. She made a mental note to speak to Sylvia when they were alone and held up the necklace.

"This isn't mine. Where in the bathroom did you find it?"

Sylvia trembled as tears welled up in her eyes anew. "It was just sitting there on the counter next to the sink. I swear I didn't take it."

Tempest rose and kneeled once again in front of the now sobbing woman. She placed a hand on her knee. "I know. This isn't an item that would be able to be stolen easily. It will always find its rightful owner. Do you know what this is?"

Sylvia shook her head.

"This is Vesper's token—the god of stars and time."

Tempest gently took Sylvia's hand and laid the necklace in her palm. It began to glow with a warm golden light.

Tempest forced a smile to her face. It seemed that at least one of the other gods had found her. If he hadn't known before, Vesper would have been notified when she came in contact with his token.

As she watched Sylvia's wide-eyed face, she couldn't help but approve of Vesper's choice. While she hadn't spent much time with the woman, her ability had been clear in its judgment that Sylvia was a woman of honor. Tempest was intrigued, though. It wasn't often that Vesper joined in Dei Electi. He was a busy and reclusive god, rarely joining in matters dealing with mortals directly.

"It appears we've found another participant of Dei Electi," Aiden said, startling both women. "Congratulations."

Sylvia stared at her emperor with a slack jaw. "Excuse me?"

Tempest chuckled. "That's what the necklace means. Vesper has claimed you as his representative."

"It's true. For the duration of Dei Electi, you will be relieved of your responsibilities, and you will move into one of the rooms in this wing. We will, of course, assist in providing anything you may need for any of the events. I'm not privy to the specific details of each event, but it is something we do to level the competition, so all participants can compete fairly."

"Oh no, this must be a mistake. There's no possible way I could have been chosen for this."

Tempest felt panic and a pang of deep sadness from Sylvia, as well as a small but surprising sense of relief.

Aiden motioned one of his guards forward. "Lin will escort you to your room. No need to be nervous."

Looking back and forth between Tempest and Aiden before standing, Sylvia muttered thanks and followed Lin out of the room. The other guards followed closely behind and, with a last glance as they took up their post outside, closed the door behind them. Tempest slid off her knees and sat fully on the floor, her mind racing.

"I will send someone to clean the rest of this up for you."

She'd forgotten that Aiden was still in the room with her for a moment. She looked up at him.

"Thank you. I appreciate that."

"I initially came to let you know that the other women should be arriving tonight. Tomorrow will be the claiming ceremony to prove that all participants are representatives of their intended gods. We need to come up with a plan."

"A plan? What for?"

"You weren't actually chosen by the goddess of the broken. It's been so long that no one remembers what her sign usually is, but we need to figure out something."

During the claiming ceremony, the participants of Dei Electi showed their tokens as proof they were chosen by the gods. The god who sponsored each of them had the opportunity to give an additional sign if they chose to do so. Tempest's abilities weren't flashy, so when she'd shown a sign for her representatives in the past, she often called out a criminal in the room and their victim. Of course, she'd had to use a little leverage to get them there in the first place, but her mark appeared on them as her representative spoke, and nothing could remove it until she willed it.

"Ah, that. I have a few ideas."

He eyed her with doubt. "Such as?"

She smirked. "Now, what fun would it be to give away all of my secrets?"

"Like how you had her token at the gate?"

While many responses were at the tip of her tongue, she decided silence and a smile would disturb him the most. Usually, tormenting someone wasn't her idea of fun—it didn't sit right with mending broken hearts—but something about bothering Emperor Aiden was amusing to her. They held each other's gaze, a challenge of wills to see who would give first.

Aiden cracked first with a laugh. "Fine, keep your secrets. I'm watching you, though."

She laughed in return. "Promises, promises. I will be ready, though. No need to worry."

CHAPTER 8

Tempest stood in the hallway outside the ballroom with the eleven other women. All of them were dressed in highly embroidered gowns; matching jewelry adorned their arms and necks, and was even woven into their hair. The women's anxiety made Tempest want to empty her stomach. It was almost suffocating to be so near to them.

A liveried man ushered the women nearer to the large double doors and signaled for them to wait as the doors were dramatically opened. He stepped into the ballroom, unrolled a scroll, and loudly announced, "Lily. Representative of Eshum, god of healing."

A short woman with fiery hair and a green and gold ensemble tentatively approached the door. She took a deep breath, then lifted her head high and entered. Polite clapping erupted from the room.

The herald spoke again. "Faith. Representative of Amias, god of love."

Tempest watched a curvy woman with large chocolate eyes framed by long lashes sashay through the entrance, her black and red gown hugging every curve. She couldn't help but laugh internally at Amias's choice. Of course he would choose a woman who practically oozed sexual appeal.

"Isabella," the herald proclaimed. "Representative of Aloysius, god of war."

The silver of daggers strapped to her thighs peeked out of the high slits in Isabella's gold dress as she walked through the doorway. Tempest made a mental note to keep a wary eye on the woman. Aloysius had been very displeased with her before she left the land of the gods. If he had selected Isabella, there was no doubt she could use those blades better than most, if not all, of the guards present.

"Mila. Representative of Bramble, goddess of fertility and harvest."

A hand grasped at Tempest's dress as Mila tripped over her own feet and began to fall. Tempest grabbed the woman's arms and caught her before she could hit the ground.

Warm green eyes peered back up at her. "I'm so sorry!"

"It's fine," Tempest replied with a smile as she pulled Mila back to her feet. "Really, don't worry about it."

As she watched the gangly woman hurry towards the doorway, Tempest analyzed the residual reading she had pulled from her. No ill will was apparent in her heart, but there was something Tempest couldn't quite put her finger on. The herald continued announcing, however, and she decided to wait until she was alone to mull it over.

"Aurora. Representative of Septimus, god of luck."

A tall blonde woman with a dress as deep a blue as her glistening eyes made her way to the entrance. With her shoulders back and a smirk on her face, Aurora appeared the most confident of the women. Tempest would bet good money this woman was from one of the noble families. Moments later, a round of approving *oohs* and *aahs* followed by enthusiastic clapping was heard from the ballroom.

"Sylvia. Representative of Vesper, god of stars and time."

Tempest caught Sylvia's eye and sent her a reassuring smile. She looked beautiful in her sapphire blue gown. Silver stars were embroidered across it in constellations that matched the night sky. Sylvia seemed the most nervous of the representatives. As a servant who had always been taught that her place was away from the spotlight, Tempest could understand why.

As soon as Sylvia neared the ballroom, everything went dark. Gasps and cries could be heard from both those in the hall and in the ballroom. A small, golden star flickered into being above Sylvia's head, followed by a crescent moon that nestled the star in its crook. With a smile that finally reached her eyes, Sylvia entered the ballroom and took her light with her, plunging the hallway into darkness once again.

Tempest chuckled. Vesper wouldn't be Vesper if he didn't do something so theatrical. She found it especially fitting that he made his representative be allowed to feel as if, at this moment, she was alone. He hid the crowd from someone who wasn't equipped to handle them.

Soon the darkness receded, and the next woman was called forward.

"Luna. Representative of Ruyah, goddess of sleep and dreams."

A willowy woman with long white hair slipped between the remaining women in the hall. Her footsteps were silent as she passed them by.

"Serenity. Representative of Tynan, god of chaos and luck."

Tempest snorted, earning in a dirty look from the dark-skinned woman as she began her way to the doorway. Tynan wasn't a god Tempest had ever found to be funny, but the irony of a representative named Serenity surely couldn't have been missed, even by him.

As soon as she walked through the doorway, one of the remaining women mumbled, "Wasn't there already a god of luck?"

They all glanced at each other and shrugged.

"Tynan is the god of chaos and luck. His luck isn't always good," Tempest explained. "Septimus is the god of *good* luck. Technically, Tynan is more powerful than Septimus, since he can answer more prayers that are sent to him. The more worshipers a god has, the more power they have to answer prayers with. Good luck takes more power and energy to give, so Septimus isn't as powerful of a god. Many of those prayers go unanswered."

A woman with hair so black it almost looked blue cocked her head to the side. "Are you a temple worker for one of them?"

Tempest waved her hands in front of her and quickly replied, "No, I just love learning."

The woman raised her brow and began making her way to the doorway when her name was called.

"Mya. Representative of Zarya, goddess of the sea."

Fog curled through the doorway soon after Mya entered. The gods weren't keeping it simple today. How bored they must be, if they all felt they needed to put on this much of a show.

"Gloria. Representative of Kirata, goddess of the heavens."

Eyes wide, Tempest whipped her head around to see who the goddess that ruled over the land of the gods had chosen. Kirata was one of the only gods Tempest feared; not because she was an evil god, but because she was one of the only ones strong enough to drag her back. It was unusual for her to send a representative.

A lean but toned woman with caramel hair and amber eyes walked towards the doorway without even a glance at the rest of them. Clapping and cheering followed her entrance to the ballroom.

Tempest looked at the last woman standing in the hallway. The gold dress, golden hair, and warm skin tone immediately told her who this woman represented.

"Alina. Representative of Soleil, goddess of the sun."

Tempest circled her thumbs around each other as she waited her turn. Soleil was flashy, so her sign took longer than the rest.

"Tempest. Representative of Tempest, goddess of the broken."

Head held high, she straightened the simple white dress she had chosen and made her way into the ballroom.

A pedestal stood at the end of the walkway. Aiden sat on his throne on the other side of it. Golden embroidery covered his dark blue uniform; he looked as stiff as the uniform must have felt. Three men in black with long swords hanging from their hips stood behind and on either side of him.

A man in purple finery waited for Tempest at the pedestal. Well over a hundred pairs of eyes followed her progress down the unmarked aisle. She pulled her token out of her pocket as she approached and placed it on the sandstone with a soft clink.

The man in purple spoke. "What proof do you present that your token is true?"

Tempest locked eyes with Aiden and grinned wickedly. "The blood of the guilty."

Chapter 9

Tempest slowly spun to show all who were in the room what she was doing. Unlike the other representatives, she wore no jewelry or shoes. She wanted nothing to draw attention away from the message she would send today.

Her dress slowly turned from white to crimson, the color bleeding from her collar downward until her entire gown was saturated. She could have left it at that. The gasps in the room told her that she had already done enough to pass the test. This moment would be wasted if she stopped now, though. She slowly walked around the pedestal and picked up her token, facing Aiden again. Red dripped from the hem and train of her dress onto the stone floor, painting a wet trail as her feet left dark footprints behind her.

Tempest stretched her arms out to the crowd. "I give you the blood of the guilty and a promise from the goddess of the broken," she pronounced, then fastened her eyes on the man on the throne. "No harm will come to you, Emperor Aiden; only to those who wish to harm you."

Aiden showed no sign of acknowledgment as Tempest turned to join the other women participating in Dei Electi, though he held her gaze steadily. She wondered what the high and mighty emperor thought of her display. From the uneasy shuffling of the crowd to the shocked and horrified faces of the other representatives, Tempest knew her point had reached those she'd intended it for.

Tempest walked to the end of the line of women and turned to face the crowd. Alina inched towards the other girls, trying to create more space between them. Tempest couldn't blame her. Her dress was still staining the ground around her.

The ballroom was silent until the purple-adorned man in the center came to his senses. "There you have it. Our twelve participants of this generation's Dei Electi. Emperor, do you accept the gods' offerings?"

Aiden's eyes were still locked on Tempest. "I do."

"And with that, ladies and gentlemen, let the feast begin! Ladies of the Dei Electi, welcome."

Servants entered with trays of food and drinks and started circulating among the crowd. Music began to play, conversations were initiated, and the other women of Dei Electi hurried away from Tempest as quickly as they could, whispering amongst themselves. Only Sylvia remained.

"That was incredible!" she said as she drew near Tempest. The sparkle in her eyes hadn't dimmed since her entrance. "I've never heard of a god offering a threat… no, promise? Whatever that was, before. What was it like having her speak to you? Vesper hasn't said a word. I was terrified it was all a big mistake right up until I started to glow."

Tempest laughed. "Don't be too offended if he doesn't speak to you. It's unusual for a god to interact directly with a mortal, even their representative."

"You've been studying up on past Dei Electis, as well? I stayed up all night reading anything and everything I could find on them."

"I like to read. What can I say?," Tempest replied with a shrug. "You certainly seem to be feeling better, though."

Sylvia was practically bouncing on the balls of her feet. "I feel… at peace. I'm sure it won't last long, but I'm enjoying it while I've got it."

"I completely understand. I…"

Tempest to pause when someone coughed behind her, clearly asking for her attention. She turned to find Aiden standing there, his arm outstretched.

"Would you like to join me for the first dance?"

Tempest gestured to her dress. "You aren't afraid I will stain your uniform?"

He chuckled. "If this gets ruined, I'm sure I can find another."

With a quick smile back toward her new friend, Tempest took Aiden's hand. The two of them made their way to the center of the room, and the musicians began a new tune. With his hand on her back and their opposite ones adjoined, they began to sway and step to the rhythm.

"I need to know. How did you do that?"

"Do what, Emperor Aiden?"

"Your dress. It's dripping blood."

"Really? Are you sure?"

Aiden spun her out and paused before spinning her back in.

"Okay, I really need to know how you did that."

"Did what?"

"How is your dress white again? And completely dry!"

Tempest allowed a coy smile to spread across her face. "A lady can never reveal her secrets."

"A lady?"

"Am I not?"

He regarded her for a moment. "Honestly, I'm not sure. I really don't know anything about you."

More couples joined the dance, and soon a crowd was gathered around them.

"I am at your disposal for approximately two more minutes and thirty-seven seconds," Tempest said. "What would you like to know?"

"Tell me about your family."

"I don't know them. I've been alone for as long as I can remember."

"You're an orphan? Were you homeless?"

"I didn't say that. I just don't know who my family is."

"You're not giving me much here, you know. Maybe we can try something simple. What's your favorite food?"

"That's easy. Dandelion shortbread cookies."

Aiden's nose scrunched. "The weed? Isn't it incredibly sticky and bitter? I swear, you touch it, and your hands smell of it for hours. How could you possibly enjoy those?"

"Revealing one of your flaws, are you? Unable to see how there could be anything positive about something that seems so bitter? If you only use the yellow center, it's sweet and almost tastes like honey. You should try them sometime."

"I'm sure our cooks would appreciate the request for what I am assuming is a commoner recipe."

"It doesn't matter how much something costs or how rare it is. If it's tasty, I'm not turning my nose up at it."

"Point taken. I will make sure to keep that in mind."

Aiden's hand shifted on her back as he dipped her at the conclusion of the song. Through the connection that Fate had given them, Tempest could feel joy in his heart. For a moment, she almost wished she could actually be one of the women competing to share his throne. She knew the heartbreak that would be waiting for her at the other end of his short lifespan, though, and highly doubted the other gods would let her go so easily now that they had found her. No, she needed to complete her mission and escape as quickly as she could.

CHAPTER 10

Tempest followed her nose the next morning to find the dining room. Fresh coffee, some sort of sweet baked good, and bacon had awoken her, mouth-watering and fully alert.

While she didn't need to sleep, she could choose to when it served her. After her dance and conversation with Aiden the night before, she needed a moment of peace from the overanalyzing thoughts in her head. She didn't know why what he said affected her so much. The only conclusion she could come to was that Fate must have something to do with this. Did they hate her so much that they would force her heart to choose someone who would soon slip through her fingers and turn to dust? Her fists clenched at the thought. These sorts of games were precisely why she had left the land of the gods.

All too soon, the dining hall was directly in front of her. After a quick adjustment of the skirt over the pants she hid underneath, she entered, heading first for the table piled high with trays of food.

Giggles from the end of the long table echoed in the large room. Without turning her head, Tempest glanced towards the sound to find Aiden at its head and all of the other women as close to him as possible. All but Sylvia, who sat at the far end away from the crowd with her eyes closed, grinning from ear to ear as she chewed her food.

Turning towards the table with a now full plate and a cup of black coffee, Tempest considered her options. As tempting as taking her food back to her room was, a letter had been delivered last night that said the first trial of Dei Electi would be discussed at breakfast. Decision made, she joined Sylvia, who cracked an eye open when she arrived.

"Have you ever had such delicious coffee?" Sylvia asked.

Tempest shook her head. "I haven't had a chance to try it yet."

"Oh!" Sylvia laughed. "I got ahead of myself. Even though I've worked here most of my life, we never get to try the good coffee. Too expensive to spend on the likes of the servants."

Tempest nodded while Sylvia chatted away and took a sip of coffee. A hint of nutmeg, cinnamon, and vanilla teased her taste buds, softening the bitter drink.

"Did you not add sugar or cream?"

"I actually prefer it without."

Eyes wide, Sylvia glanced at the cup of coffee in front of her. "You can't be serious."

Tempest took another sip. "Dead serious. It balances the sweetness of the foods I most often consume with it."

Sylvia continued to speak while Tempest picked at her plate, replying half-heartedly when needed. The food was good, but the people in the room were of more interest to her. Most of the representatives had come with companions, who lined the room's walls in small groups, talking quietly amongst themselves.

As she looked over the women sitting around Aiden, a pair of golden eyes locked with hers. The chatter in the room muted. She darted a glance at a hand as it touched his sleeve, his name falling from the lips of the woman it belonged to. Tempest looked back at Aiden's face to find that he was still watching her, completely ignoring the other woman.

She smirked and lifted her head as she turned her attention back to Sylvia and the food on her plate. A voice in her head called her bluff as she told herself that the butterflies she felt were in his stomach and not her own.

"If I can have your attention, please."

The room fell silent as all eyes turned toward Eb, the noble from the courtyard when she first arrived.

"Congratulations on being chosen to compete in the Dei Electi. One of you lucky women will be our next empress!"

The nervous and excited emotions in the room quickly rose with his words, giving Tempest a sudden headache. Holding her head in her hand, she placed her elbow on the table and breathed deeply in an attempt to keep her breakfast down.

"The first trial will be held today," Eb continued. "You are expected to be at the entrance to the south gate within the hour. If you are late, you will be disqualified."

The room was silent but for Eb's footsteps as he exited the room without further explanation. As soon as he left, chairs scraped and urgent chatter filled the room as the representatives and their companions quickly left to prepare.

Tempest's headache eased as the crowd, and their emotions, moved further away. She looked up to find herself almost alone. Only a few guards, servants cleaning up, and the emperor, who stood behind Sylvia's empty chair, were left.

"Are you well?"

She buried her shaking hands in her skirt and rose from her seat. "I'm fine."

Aiden looked her over with a raised brow. "Are you prepared?"

She lifted the bottom of her skirt to reveal the trousers beneath and replied, "I came prepared."

Aiden smirked. "Of course, you did."

Tempest shrugged as she turned on her heel and headed towards the exit. "I'm always prepared."

She felt his eyes follow her as she left the room. A shiver of excitement ran up her spine. Was it because he was watching her, or because the trials were about to start? She didn't know, but something told her things were about to get interesting.

CHAPTER 11

Tempest had assumed she would be the first at the gate, but was surprised to find Sylvia already leaning against the wall from her seat on the ground. The only other people nearby were the guards patrolling along the top. Tempest sat beside Sylvia with her legs outstretched.

"I didn't expect you to already be here."

Sylvia startled. "When did you get here?"

"Just now. I didn't have much preparing to do."

Sylvia frowned. "This will most likely be a physical challenge; probably a maze with dangerous obstacles to overcome."

Tempest expected the same. It was the pattern Dei Electi usually followed and was why she'd chosen to wear pants under her dress. While she was difficult to injure, sliding on gravel with bare skin, jumping through flames, or many of the other possibilities for this trial would still be uncomfortable otherwise.

Tempest gave her warmest smile and nudged Sylvia's shoulder with her own. "Cheer up. You're here on time, have more endurance than most of these women due to your time as a servant, and, best of all, you have me."

"You?"

"Only if you want. We can do this together."

Sylvia gave Tempest a quick glance. "You aren't armed, either."

Tempest spread her empty hands. "Nope. I don't need them; neither do you."

Sylvia only sighed in reply.

"Afraid you would be left behind?"

Serenity and Isabella laughed as if what Gloria had said was the funniest thing they'd heard that morning. The approaching women wore strategically-placed light armor over their long dresses with daggers and short swords strapped over it. Tempest wasn't surprised that the representatives of the gods of chaos and war and the goddess of the heavens had banded together. The gods themselves had always been close, as well.

Sylvia groaned as she tucked her knees to her chest. Tears already rimmed her eyes.

"Nope," Tempest said. "Just already prepared and a bit bored waiting for everyone."

Isabella rested her hand on the short sword at her hip and smirked. "You know that this will be dangerous, right? Neither of you looks prepared in the slightest."

Tempest leaned back and rested her head on the wall. "We'll see."

Serenity squatted down and cocked her head to one side. "You do know the first round usually has at least one or two of the competitors die, right? My bet is on you two."

Tempest let her head roll to match Serenity's angle and heaved a bored sigh. "The gods don't allow their representatives to die during Dei Electi. Not unless they did something to be cast aside, that is. That's only happened a handful of times, and usually it's not during the first round."

Serenity stood back up and kicked sand as she turned around in a huff. "Whatever. You won't last long anyway."

Tempest brushed the sand off her dress as the three women walk away.

"I'm going to die," Sylvia whimpered, her head tucked into her knees.

"You're not going to die. Your god has not abandoned you. Those harpies wouldn't have put on such a big show for you if you had been."

Sylvia sniffled, and the two sat in silence as the rest of the competitors gradually arrived. All of the other women wore armor and were armed in one way or another. As tempting as giving Sylvia a weapon was, Tempest knew that it would do her no good without proper training to go with it. No, Tempest would just have to keep her as close as possible and protect her.

Her connection with Aiden felt decidedly less strained, until she knew, without a doubt, that he was standing on top of the wall directly above her.

As tempting as it was to look up and see if she could spot him, she kept her gaze on the other women, watching for any odd behaviors or signs that they may not be entirely as they seemed.

The gate groaned as it slowly opened.

"The first event has officially begun," someone announced from above the gate—Eb, if Tempest weren't mistaken. "Find a golden feather of truth, an amulet of chaos, and a ring of war before you reach the end of the maze. Good luck, Dei Electi contestants. May you remain in your god's favor."

The representatives rushed the gate as Sylvia and Tempest rose to their feet. Tempest grabbed Sylvia's hand and shook her head when she tried to join the women passing them.

"You don't want to be the first to enter. Let *them* walk into the traps and trigger them. We will follow after."

Sylvia only nodded as they took less-hurried steps through the gate's large opening. Another wall stood only three giant steps in front of them, creating a tall and narrow alleyway.

Tempest was already on high alert. She found it very concerning that no rules had been laid out for this. This wasn't right. Usually, the trials began with a long speech and regulations.

"Which way should we go?" Sylvia asked.

Nothing in either direction suggested which was the correct way to go. To the left, an opening in the wall led further into the maze, while the avenue to the right split off in several directions.

"This way," Tempest said, motioning left.

"Are you sure?"

"Not in the slightest, but we only have one decision to make if we go this way," Tempest pointed out, "compared to several if we head the other way."

Deciding that was reason enough, Sylvia caught up to Tempest, and they walked together into the maze.

Tempest chose to continue going left at every turn, only changing course if they could hear the other competitors in that direction. The loud roars of beasts, clashing of metal on metal, and screams grew more frequent the further they went. To their surprise, they didn't encounter any of the challenges that the other women appeared to have stumbled on.

Tempest's gut turned. "This is too easy."

"You think so, too?" Sylvia asked as she peeked down an alley they passed by.

"Either your god has made you very lucky—a possibility, considering your sponsor is the god of time—or something perilous is waiting for us, possibly even hunting us."

Sylvia grasped Tempest's sleeve. "Do you really think so?"

Tempest nodded as they made their next turn.

Sylvia stopped suddenly, pulling Tempest to a halt as well. "Do you see that?"

"See what?"

"The shadow."

Looking around, Tempest didn't notice anything unique about the shadows.

Sylvia let go of her sleeve and walked back to the turn they'd last taken. "I'm right. It's different."

Tempest joined her and compared the two. It appeared the shadow of one wall had grown longer than the one on the other side of the alley. Looking up the length of the walk, it seemed to beckon them forward.

"There's something over there."

"Maybe where one of the tokens is hidden?"

They smiled at each other.

"Sylvia, maybe you are lucky. There's only one way to find out. Let's go."

They picked up their pace and chose turns that took them into alleys with longer shadows. Eventually, a tile roof began to show above the top of the walls. They had to be getting close to whatever it was, and Tempest really hoped that Sylvia was lucky after all. Despite knowing that competitors rarely died, she did not like the chances that they could be very, very wrong about what was at the end of the path they followed. With Sylvia by her side, she didn't dare call for Soulshadow; it would give her identity away.

Suddenly a tall building appeared, tucked inside a courtyard through an opening in the alley. The sound of grinding stone immediately came from behind them as the two women stepped through the opening. Tempest whipped around to see the stone wall close off the last of the gap that had been there only moments before. A quick look around the courtyard revealed no other openings. They were trapped.

Chapter 12

"What do we do?" Sylvia's voice trembled as if she was near crying again.

Tempest walked cautiously towards the building. "I'm not sure yet."

The sandstone walls held no windows, only a large, open doorway leading into the dark interior.

"You can't glow again like you did last night, can you?" Tempest remarked.

Sylvia released a nervous chuckle. "I wish. I hate the dark almost as much as I hate the feeling of being trapped."

Before entering, Tempest investigated the stones of the doorway for any markings. Maybe there would be a clue about any traps inside or a way to light their way. She brushed her fingers against the swirls and circles etched into the stone, then stopped and moved her hand back over an irregularly shaped oval. Stepping back so she could see the doorway as a whole, Tempest counted twelve of them in the frame. Tempest approached one of the ovals and put her hand over it again.

"Does this feel different to you?"

Sylvia approached and swiped her fingers over it. "It feels... warm."

"It does, doesn't it?"

Moving her fingers again, Tempest touched several other ovals. "They all do. I wonder..."

Tempest tapped on the oval. A small piece of sandstone fell away to reveal a hint of black underneath. If this was what she thought it was, she dreaded what they would find inside.

She began to chip away at the sandstone to reveal more black underneath. Seeing what she was doing, Sylvia did the same with another oval. Soon, the thin layer coating revealed an entirely black stone underneath. Tempest mentally kicked herself for not bringing a blade with her as she dug her nails around the edges and pried it out of the wall.

"It's an egg!" Sylvia exclaimed, her voice raising a few octaves. Her fingers scrabbled at the edges of the egg she had been uncovering, and soon she too held one in her now bloody hands.

"Shake it slightly and press your fingers against it to seal the scrapes on your fingertips."

Sylvia did as Tempest suggested and hissed when her egg grew hot. "How do I get it to cool back down now?"

Tempest shook hers with a small groan. "You don't. We need them hot so they can glow and light our way within. Phoenix eggs that will soon hatch heat up when you upset the hatchling inside."

Sylvia's jaw dropped as she looked back and forth between her now-glowing egg and Tempest. "You've got to be kidding me."

"I wish I was."

"You don't think..."

Tempest nodded. "Unfortunately, I do think."

Sylvia stared at her egg a moment and lifted the bottom of her dress, dropping the egg within the fold she had created. "All right, then. At least if it's going to be this hot to touch, we don't have to carry it with our bare hands."

"At least, not until your dress catches on fire."

Sylvia's eyes grew wider before a look of determination settled on her face. "We will cross that bridge when we have to." With a deep breath, she turned and entered the dark building.

Tempest was right on her heels. Soon the light from the doorway faded away, and they could only see each other's outlines in the dim glow of their eggs.

Sylvia suddenly stumbled, and Tempest grabbed the back of her dress to catch her. She pulled her upright, and they looked down. A staircase descended into the darkness below them.

With nowhere else to go, Tempest tested the first few steps. The constant stillness troubled her. What was waiting for them ahead? She decided the stairs were safe, and they descended.

A welcome green and blue glow rippled across the walls as they entered an underground cavern. A small pool of water with glowing stones lining the bottom sat in the middle of the room, surrounded by four pedestals, each with a different size and shape of bowl placed atop it. One bowl was large, gold, and embellished with bright red rubies. Another was made of smooth crystal. The one nearest them had been carved from white marble, with wings etched along the rim. The last bowl was bright green jade with golden veins running through it.

Tempest approached the pool and looked within. A wooden ladle and bucket floated at the edge. A hand grabbed her wrist as she reached for them, and a woman composed of water arose.

"This pool is as pure as your heart must be to take from it," she crooned. "The bowls will be your judge. Choose carefully, or this place on your search for the feather of fate may become your tomb."

The woman removed her hand from Tempest's wrist and offered her a private smile. The daughter of Zarya, goddess of the sea, and Eshum, god of healing, this sprite had been born of a fleeting love. Cast aside once it was over, Tempest had helped her rectify her broken heart. While Tempest most often helped with scorned lover, the broken heart of a child was something she couldn't ignore. She was tempted to ask the sprite how she had come to be in the cave, but chose to be silent instead.

"So, we need to put water in a bowl to get out of here?" Sylvia asked.

"It sounds like it," Tempest answered as she dipped the bucket to fill it and set the ladle within. "I'm guessing only one will get us out of here. The rest are likely boobytrapped—the cave collapses, the pool floods the room, the stairs seal off, and we get trapped in here; that sort of thing."

She glanced back at her sprite friend, who gave her a nod in return. It appeared her assessment was correct.

"Do you think we'll die? Like, really die, if we chose the wrong one?"

"To be honest, I'm not sure. I would rather not find out, though."

"Agreed." Sylvia fidgeted with the hem of her skirt, careful not to drop the egg as she approached each bowl. "Which one do you think it is?"

Tempest shifted her egg under her arm, afraid it would be lost if she set it down, and considered the bowls. "This is for the feather of fate, so what would best represent that?"

Sylvia stopped at the golden bowl. "Perhaps this one? It is a golden feather, after all."

"I don't know. Fate isn't flashy. That's by far the most over-the-top one in here."

"You're right." Sylvia walked over to the bowl made of white marble. "What about this? It could represent that we should be pure of heart like she said we needed to be."

Tempest thought for a moment. "I feel as if that bowl is a trap. Fate isn't truly pure. Their hands are covered in blood. And rarely are those who think they are pure actually without blemish."

"That makes sense. I suppose that leaves these two," Sylvia mused as she moved on.

Tempest tried to understand what the bowls communicated about fate as she looked at them. She had to remind herself that this wasn't an actual test from Fate itself, but rather from what a mortal designing the trial had decided fate was. Most mortals didn't understand that Fate was, in fact, an actual being and not just a force of nature. While not even the gods knew who Fate was, they did know that they were a living being.

"Everything is known and nothing is hidden from fate," Tempest began, "so it could be the clear crystal bowl. On the other hand, fate is unpredictable and often mends that which is broken. The jade bowl has been repaired with the gold, sealing it together."

She glanced at the sprite, hoping for a clue, but found no help, only a reassuring smile.

Sylvia walked to both bowls and investigated more closely. "Which one do you think it is?"

"I'm honestly not sure," Tempest said as she weighed the options in her mind. "Why don't you decide?"

Sylvia gaped at Tempest. "I couldn't! What if I guessed wrong?"

"Your guess is as good as mine."

She watched as Sylvia made up her mind. While Tempest knew which one she would choose, the fact that this was a trial made by a mortal and not Fate itself made her hesitate. Having a mortal make the decision was her best bet to get this right—or so she hoped.

"It's the crystal bowl."

"You're sure?"

"Of course not! Your reasoning for it just makes more sense to me. Especially for a test from nobles who will want an empress to think she is always being watched and that she cannot escape judgment for her actions."

Tempest's eyebrows rose. She hadn't considered that. She would have chosen the jade bowl, but found Sylvia's reasoning to be sound.

"I agree."

She carried the bucket of water to the crystal bowl and took a deep breath before pouring some in.

Chapter 13

Tempest and Sylvia dropped to their knees and protected the eggs with their bodies as the ground began to shake. Dust and small rocks fell in the room. For a moment, Tempest was sure they had guessed wrong.

The shaking stopped as quickly as it began, and a melodic laugh reached them from the pool. "You may arise. Both of you have passed this challenge."

Sylvia looked up, still hunched over her egg. "We did?"

"Yes, you did. While your reasonings were...informative, the bowls were not actually your test. The eggs were."

Tempest pulled her egg out from under her and held it up. "How were the eggs our test?"

"You protected it over yourself. Both of you put the life of another ahead of your own."

Tempest wasn't reassured, and the sinking feeling in her gut returned.

"And how exactly is that related to fate?" she asked.

The sprite laughed again. “I’m afraid I am not permitted to reveal that at this time. I suggest you continue through that opening,” she said, pointing to an opening that had appeared when the room shook, “and claim your reward before the others arrive. Several other potential empresses have recently entered the building.”

Sylvia rose, cradling her egg in her skirt again, while Tempest put the bucket and ladle back in the pool.

“Thank you,” Tempest said to the water sprite.

The sprite smiled and melted back into the still water.

The room began to shake again, and Tempest and Sylvia ran through the opening before it closed again. A blast of heat hit them, and Sylvia instantly broke out in a sweat. A large golden bird sat in the middle of the room in a large nest.

Tentatively, the two approach the bird and set the eggs in the nest with its mother. They quickly backed away as the phoenix squawked loudly and nuzzled the eggs.

“It feels good to have reunited a mother with...*what*?!” Sylvia cried out as the phoenix crushed both eggs under her large talons and flew off to a perch above.

Tempest’s shoulders slumped. This was the Fate she knew—unpredictable, and often unfair. “The mother rejected them because we touched them.

They must have been just shy of hatching and at their bonding stage."

Sylvia released a sob. "They can bond before they hatch?"

Tempest nodded and quietly approached the nest to see if there was any chance the hatchlings had survived. To her surprise, two gold feathers lay in the shells of the crushed eggs. She pulled them from the nest and held them up.

"It appears we have found the golden feathers of fate."

Sylvia wiped the tears from her face as she approached. She reached out to grab one of the feathers. The moment her fingers grasped it, they were instantly transported into the maze once again.

"What just happened?"

"It appears we have completed the trial of fate."

Sylvia nodded. "Where are we, though?"

Tempest looked around. To her surprise, the building they had just been in was nowhere to be found. Even its shadow was gone. "I'm guessing in the trial of chaos."

"I don't like the sound of that."

"The sooner we start, the sooner we get out of here."

They navigated through the narrow alleys of the maze, once again choosing to take mostly left turns. This time there were no sounds of the other women meeting challenges. Only the soft padding of their footsteps and the occasional beast's snarls in nearby alleys reached their ears.

"I don't like this," Sylvia whimpered.

Before Tempest could reply, a lion slunk around the corner and crouched before them. Both women froze, afraid to move. The beast roared and charged at them anyway.

Tempest pushed Sylvia out of its path and gripped its fur as it landed on top of her. It's teeth snapped near her neck, only held at bay by her immortal strength. She pulled her feet under the beast and, with a mighty push, rolled it off of her and flung it a few feet away, where it landed on its back.

She darted a glance at Sylvia. The woman sprawled out on the ground, blood trickling from her temple. Before she could approach to see if there was breath in her body, the lion was back on its feet and charging again.

Tempest dodged, pushed against the wall with her feet, and swung herself onto the back of the lion. Soulshadow appeared at her fingertips, and she swung it around the neck of the beast. It reared onto its hind legs as its roar was abruptly cut off.

Falling to its side, the beast thrashed, crushing Tempest's leg under it as she tightened Soulshadow's chain until it eventually fell limp. She held her grip a moment longer to ensure the beast was, in fact, dead before pulling herself away from it and allowing Soulshadow to disappear.

Tempest pushed the lion off herself and ran to Sylvia's side. Her heart sank as she realized her chest wasn't moving. She placed two fingers on her wrist to check for a pulse, but found none. Anger welled up within her, and she released an angry cry as her fist pounded the wall. A large crack spread from where she'd hit it.

She hadn't realized she'd struck Sylvia so hard. Her only intent was to protect the woman, not harm her. Definitely not to kill her.

Dropping to her knees, Tempest lifted Sylvia's head into her lap. She rocked back and forth while stroking the woman's hair, tears spilling onto her graying skin.

How had she let herself become so attached to a mortal? She hadn't even had the chance to find out who had wronged Sylvia. The only person here who was kind to Tempest with no ulterior motive was now gone. Honestly, she barely knew the woman, but she felt as if she had let her down all the same.

Movement near Sylvia's feet caught Tempest's eye, and her fingers stopped, still tangled in Sylvia's hair. A red snake slowly slithered up Sylvia's legs, making its way towards her. Tempest moved to grab and kill the snake when suddenly she stopped. At the top of its head sat a moon and star nestled together.

"I thought you had abandoned your representative, Vesper."

The snake ignored her and continued moving up Sylvia's body.

While no god could transform themselves into another being, some could temporarily create one for their purposes or possess a lower life form. She contemplated which Vesper had done as she watched the snake slither up Sylvia's chest and strike her neck. Its fangs sank deep in her flesh for a few moments before it withdrew and slithered away.

Tempest watched with bated breath until Sylvia gasped and rolled to her side. She moved away as Sylvia retched onto the sand. Once her stomach was empty of all of its contents, Sylvia rolled onto her back and breathed deeply with her eyes closed.

"Are you all right?" Tempest asked.

Sylvia took a few moments to answer. "I feel terrible."

"Well, you were just dead."

Sylvia's eyes snapped open. "I was what?"

Realizing her mistake too late, Tempest relayed the last few minutes to a shocked Sylvia.

"So, he really did choose me."

"It appears you hold Vesper's favor."

Sylvia groaned as she pulled herself up into a sitting position. "How do you know so much stuff?"

"I don't know about everything."

Sylvia cocked her head and scrutinized Tempest. "Pretty close."

The pair eyed each other. Finally, Tempest rose and offered a hand.

"We should get going before something else finds us."

Sylvia clasped her hand and swayed as she rose. "You're right. We should get going."

"Are you sure you're all right?"

"Yep, just a little nauseous."

"Being dead and then bit by a snake can do that to you."

"Excuse me?"

"Too soon?"

Sylvia stared at Tempest a moment longer before cracking a small smile. "You know, I always liked you. I think we're going to be good friends."

Tempest was afraid to admit it, but for the first time in a long time, she had let her guard down enough that Sylvia may be right.

"Let's get going. Do you need to lean on me?"

Sylvia took a few slow steps forward. "I don't think so. Not yet, at least."

With a last look over her new friend, Tempest led the way down the alley, setting a much slower pace than before. Several minutes later, Sylvia was already panting and leaning on the wall.

"I'm sorry, I need just a minute to rest."

Sweat had broken out on Sylvia's brow, and Tempest didn't like how pale she looked.

"I can carry you if needed."

"Not yet. I just need a moment."

Tempest stood near Sylvia, watching her friend's labored breathing and keeping an eye out for any threat. If this was the chaos portion of the maze, they couldn't be too careful. Oh, how she wished they could just find the amulets of chaos and get out of there.

As if in answer to her thoughts, an older man hopped down from the top of the wall walked towards them.

Sylvia looked up, still leaning on the wall, whimpered. “No. Not you. Why are you here?”

As he approached, a wicked smirk spread on the man’s face. “You didn’t think you could avoid me, did you? Not even participating in the Dei Electi can save you. Do you really think being empress will let you escape?”

The man stopped in front of Sylvia and reached up to brush her cheek. “No, being empress just means you will be trapped here with me forever.”

Sylvia slid down the wall, covering her face with her hands.

Tempest’s fist connected with the man’s jaw. It sank into it as if she was hitting risen dough and came out cleanly on the other side. She retracted her arm in horror.

"What are you?" Tempest asked as she shielded Sylvia with her body.

“She knows who I am.”

Tempest snarled and threw a smidge of her power into her voice. “I doubt that. You’re not a mortal man. I’ll ask again, what are you?”

The man’s appearance rippled for a moment, revealing a small being made of a reflective material inside before becoming solid again.

"Ah, I see. You're an opprob."

The man's face shifted from a sneer to shock as her fist entered his chest and came in contact with the being inside. He completely disappeared as she wrapped her fingers around its body and squeezed, shattering its glass body into tiny mirror pieces that fell to the ground.

Tempest squatted down and faced Sylvia. "It's all right now, he's gone."

Peeking between her fingers first, Sylvia slowly removed her still shaking hands from her face. "Where did he go?"

Pointing to the mirror shards behind her, Tempest replied, "He was never really here."

Sylvia shifted to her knees and crawled over to the pieces. She hesitantly reached out to touch one. Tempest saw a flicker in the remnants of the mirror just before Sylvia's finger came in contact with it and cried out, but she was too late. Sylvia was gone.

Tempest grabbed a fistful of sand and threw it at the shards in front of her.

"*Why?!*"

She allowed herself to fall on her rear and laid back on the ground. She allowed tears to roll down her face as she stared at the sky. Tempest had promised to protect Sylvia throughout this trial, and not only had killed her, but also lost her.

Tempest closed her eyes and took a deep breath, forcing herself to accept that this was Fate. Not just fate as the mortals understood it; it was clear to her that Fate, the ambiguous entity, was involved, as well.

She was done.

She wouldn't, and couldn't, do this anymore. If Fate wanted something from her, they would need to either be more clear or find someone else.

Time dragged on as she lay there. She didn't care. Too many minutes to track passed before she noticed a weight on her chest. Unwilling to open her eyes, she lifted her hand to investigate. Cold metal greeted her fingers.

She opened her eyes and lifted the object above her face. A silver amulet? She brought it closer and read the tiny inscription.

Only by understanding your fate and embracing chaos can you truly know what it is to rule.

Tempest sat up, and looked at her surroundings. While the walls looked the same as before, the mirror shards were gone. As she peered further down the path, she realized that she must have completed the maze of chaos.

She chuckled to herself as she rose and brushed the dust off her now filthy dress. There were several competitors that she imagined would have difficulty with this challenge. Only by abandoning reason and giving up on trying to 'solve' the maze had she been able to find her way out.

A quick look at the blazing sun overhead told her that it was nearing midday. She hadn't been in the trial as long as she'd thought.

Hanging the amulet around her neck, Tempest set off to tackle the maze of war. She felt more prepared for this portion than the previous ones. After all, she was no stranger to war.

Chapter 14

The pain in her chest was making it difficult to breathe. Wherever this maze was, it was very far away from Aiden; further than she liked. She needed to hurry and finish.

To her surprise, she found a dead end behind her and only one opening out of the alley she was in front of. The exit opened into a vast space.

Mounds of gold and jewels were piled in the center of the area. Deep ditches filled with scalding coals skirted the edge. Jagged pillars reached up through the embers like stakes ready for the condemned.

Tempest doubted obtaining the ring would be as simple as digging into this pile of treasure to find it. The ground trembled, and the treasure shifted to reveal a form previously hidden beneath it.

Brown and yellow scales as well as leathery sections of hide peeked through the mounded wealth. If she had to hazard a guess, Tempest was looking at a sand dragon asleep in its hoard. She couldn't imagine how the Dei Electi officials had gotten one here along with its hoard. Not even the gods dared take on a dragon without care.

She reexamined the ditches and pillars. It appeared that she had two options—attempt to sneak into the piled treasure and search through it for one of the rings, or use the pillars to skirt around the dragon. Tempest doubted the rings were actually in the hoard itself, but thought it likely they were hidden on the other side of it.

Tempest crept onto the narrow ledge that stretched between the entrance and the dragon's hoard. She walked to one far edge of it, then turned and sprinted the four steps it took to reach the other end, launching herself towards the nearest column.

Her fingers gripped the warm stone as she slid down it until her foot caught on a tiny projection, stopping her fall moments before landing in the hot coals below.

She had been merely concerned that her clothing would be burned, but the amount of heat radiating from the too-near coals told her that she may not survive, or at least would be severely injured, if she fell.

Tempest climbed up the column and jumped to the next one. She fell short of the top and again slid until she found hand- and footholds. Slowly, repeating the same scenario at each pillar, she made her way around the inferno surrounding the hoard. After what felt like an age, only three pillars remained between her and the end.

Ignoring her injuries and mangled clothing, she completely focused on her task, and with a grunt, she launched herself at the next column. Just as her hands gripped the stone, a bolt of lightning struck it.

The pillar immediately crumbled in a deafening explosion. Tempest screamed as she flailed in the air, attempting to grab onto anything that may remain. The scorching coals quickly greeted her.

Her flesh immediately blistered and peeled. She scrambled to the edge and attempted to climb out, but the hot coals slid beneath her like stones in a fiery river.

A roar drowned out her screams, and a gust of wind pushed her deeper into the scalding ditch. Gold coins sizzled and melted as they fell off the dragon's body around her. It dove at Tempest, mouth open. It nearly snapped her up and got a mouthful of coals instead.

She tried climbing the side of the ditch again, only to slide back down and sink up to her waist. The pain was overwhelming all other senses, and her vision began to darken. Her consciousness faded in and out. Flashes of the dragon flying above and taking another dive at her alternated with moments of insensibility.

Tempest called Soulshadow to her fingers and began spinning the chain, ready to answer her call home.

Flickers of memories appeared as her mind retreated from the tumultuous present into the safety of a known past. One moment the sand dragon was coming at her, and the next, she was staring down an entire army while leading one of her own.

For the first few centuries after leaving the gods, she had avoided all wars, but at a certain point, she couldn't handle the pain of all of the broken souls war brought with it. She discovered that if she joined and even led the army of the side she found most worthy, it all ended much sooner. While the moments of pain during battle and as the spirits of the dead left this land was almost overwhelming, it was less overall than when the wars lasted for years.

The dragon and past battles alternated in her vision too fast for her to keep up. Her mind almost broken to the point of not recognizing which one was the present, she prepared herself for the stupidest, but only, plan she could come up with.

As the dragon again flew within reach, Tempest released one end of Soulshadow and allowed it to wrap around the wing. Her charred body shot out of the coals as the dragon pulled up. She smacked against the ditch wall as the dragon faltered and was drug along the side until, finally, she was free.

She let go of Soulshadow, too exhausted and injured to keep it with her anymore, and dropped to the ground. Her eyes barely opened as the dragon landed. Its hoard shook and shifted with each step as it approached her. Unable to move and unsure what was real anymore, she allowed the vibrations to lull her to sleep. If she was going to die, she might as well do it while at rest.

Tempest had never thought of how she would want to die before. Being immortal, it wasn't something that came up often. The visions of past battles still played in her mind as she lay there, for the second time that day, and accepted Fate's will.

A man's roar startled her. She peered through slitted eyes and wasn't sure what she was seeing. It appeared that her crazed mind had blended her present enemy with a past battle. It didn't make sense otherwise.

Someone was fearlessly attacking the dragon, and doing a pretty good job of it, too. Knocked off balance, the dragon toppled to its side and slid into the hot ditch. It roared as the collective heat of the coals burned the thinner parts of its leathery hide.

The man hurried towards her and stopped just short of touching her. Golden eyes pierced hers. A name crossed her fevered mind. *Aiden*. No, it couldn't be. These eyes weren't his. They were ancient, intense.

The god was back.

She must have lost consciousness, because now she felt arms around her limp body and the rhythmic motion of being carried. She tried to open her eyes, to move...to do *anything*, but her body refused. She screamed soundlessly in pain as her body was laid on the ground.

"You're safe now. Rest, goddess."

She desperately wished she could open her eyes and get a good look at the god who was using the emperor's body.

There was a thump as something dropped to the ground next to her, and everything went black once more.

Urgent voices echoed around her when she woke again. Her mind was unable to grasp what they were saying. Tempest cracked her eyes open a smidge, and blurry flashes of colors moved across her vision.

She slowly turned her head towards where the sounds came from and the blurs were moving while taking note of how quickly her body was healing. Being immortal had its benefits at times like these. She would be fully healed within a few hours. How she was going to explain that was beyond her at the moment.

Frustrated that she couldn't make any sense of what was happening around her, Tempest let the darkness retake her in the hopes that she would be healed enough to figure out what was going on the next time she woke.

"But why were they together?"

"No one knows. Has the emperor already made his decision? Is she the next empress?"

Tempest kept her eyes closed and listened to the hushed voices without moving. After an unknown amount of rest, she could again make sense of the world around her. She decided to take the opportunity to listen in on what she doubted others would dare say if they knew she was awake.

"Will you two return to your duties and stop bothering them, please?" Sylvia whispered harshly. It was a relief that she was here and seemingly well.

"Just because you were selected as one of the competitors doesn't mean you're above us, Sylvia. You're just a lowly servant like the rest of us."

Sylvia's silence told Tempest that this was not the first time she had heard this.

Tempest twitched her fingers and happily discovered that they were almost fully healed. She turned her head in the direction the women's voices and slowly opened her eyes. Even though her body felt weak, she could feel her power pulsing through it, and her mind and senses were sharp. Her gaze connected with two women towering over Sylvia. The smirks dropped from their faces as quickly as their crossed arms fell to their sides.

"Leave," Tempest commanded. So much of her power was near the surface as it mended her body that it leaked into the single, scratchy word, sending the two women scurrying out of the room. Sylvia spun around on her chair and stopped just shy of touching Tempest's arm.

"You're awake!"

The tears rimming her friend's eyes nearly brought them to Tempest's, as well.

"Do you need a drink of water, or I should go get the healers?" Sylvia rambled, only stopping because Tempest rested a hand on her own.

"I'm fine. Is he all right?"

Sylvia nodded and sniffled, "He's alive. He hasn't woken up since they found you, though. What happened?"

Tempest tensed, then focused on her connection to Aiden. She only relaxed when she realized he was nearby and seemed at peace.

"Dragon."

"What? What are you talking about? What dragon?"

Tempest coughed. "What do you mean, what dragon? How did you get past it for the final challenge?"

"There was no dragon. After we were separated, I was trapped in a dark room with taunting voices. After what felt like forever, I finally gave up and suddenly appeared in a garden with a chess board. I only had to win against one of the guards to earn the final token."

"Did anyone else run into a dragon?"

Sylvia shook her head. "They all had to do the chess game, as well."

This was strange. Why was her final challenge different from the rest of the women?

"You said he hasn't woken up yet? How long has it been?"

"They found you both outside the wall last night. It's nearly mid-day now. Your body..." Sylvia choked on a sob. "You were in such bad shape," she continued through her tears. "They didn't think you would make it."

Tempest lifted her hand to wipe a tear from Sylvia's cheek.

"I'm all right. My goddess is watching over me. See, I'm nearly healed." The image of Sylvia's lifeless body in her lap popped into her mind, and her eyes darted to the bite marks on her neck. "How are *you* feeling?"

Sylvia's hand flew to cover the wound. "I feel... a-alive. A bit strange. I know I was dead. I saw the gates of Toph, but a voice called me away from them."

Tempest smiled. "You were protected by your god, as well."

"It appears so."

The two sat in companionable silence for a few minutes before Tempest pushed herself onto her elbows and up to a sitting position.

"Do you know where they have the emperor?"

"He is in his room. No one is allowed to enter."

"I understand. I just need to check on him before I can rest and finish healing."

"How?"

"Do you know any passages that will get me close to him without being seen?"

Sylvia raised a brow. "What, exactly, is going on between you and the emperor?"

Tempest's cheeks heated as she avoided Sylvia's eyes. She wasn't used to the sensation. "Nothing."

"Uh-huh. Not buying it."

"If you help me get to him, I'll tell you what I can."

"Promise?"

"Promise."

CHAPTER 15

After making Tempest drink some broth and sneaking her out of the healing wing, Sylvia led her to a large mirror in Tempest's room. She swung it open to reveal a tunnel behind it.

"You're sure you can't glow on command?" Tempest teased in an attempt to lighten the mood. It was disconcerting that there was a hidden way into her room. Sylvia was fidgeting anxiously with her fingers as she stared at the entrance.

"Nope," Sylvia replied with a quick shake of her head.

"You don't have to come with me if you don't want to."

"Really?"

Looking into the dark tunnel, Tempest could see how someone would hesitate to enter it. No lights lit the sides, and from the looks of the cobwebs and dust, it wasn't used often.

"It's fine. I can go alone. We're less likely to get caught if you don't go with me anyways. Just tell me how to get there."

Sylvia's fists clenched before relaxing. "We are very near his rooms. It seems the emperor who had this wing built wanted the contestants close. Take the first two rights, and it will bring you directly to his room."

"That's it?"

Sylvia nodded, then shook her head. "But you can't take any candles or light in with you. It could be seen at some of the exits you pass and give you away. You'll be in the dark."

"Understood. I can do that. Sylvia?"

"Yes?"

Tempest squeezed Sylvia's hand and smiled. "Thank you."

Sylvia's shoulders relaxed as she offered a warm smile in return.

"Of course," she said, grabbing the edge of the mirror as Tempest stepped inside. "Come find me when you return. I want to make sure you get rest and whatever else you need."

With a small whoosh, Tempest was dropped into the dark. Her eyes soon adjusted, and she walked steadily through the tunnels. Even if she didn't have directions from Sylvia, the pull in her chest would have guided her towards Emperor Aiden.

As she drew near, however, the feeling changed. A sense of urgency shot down and became a sharp pain in her gut. She doubled over and gasped for breath, leaning on the wall for support. Something was wrong.

She pulled herself down the hallway, unable to fully straighten as the pain grew worse with each step. Even though she was getting closer to Aiden's room, she could feel him pulling further away.

Tempest usually kept her goddess powers tamped down, but let a fraction of it fill her now to overcome the pain. A strength and renewed energy filled her and allowed the pain to lessen to only a dull reminder and guide. Her footsteps quickened as she rose and searched for Aiden's room.

Her fingers fumbled on the stone wall until she heard a small click and the wall opened a crack. She shoved it open and went through, her concern for the emperor overriding her need for secrecy. But it didn't matter; the room was empty.

She closed the hidden door behind her, allowing the wall hanging over it to drop back into place.

Frustrated, Tempest closed her eyes and focused on her connection with Aiden. He was moving away at an alarming speed. Her best guess was that he was about to leave the castle and disappear into the streets of the capital.

She quickly unlatched the double doors and stepped out onto the balcony. She was three stories high, and a walled garden spread below her. Unsure how many walls she would have to climb over or how many guards she would need to avoid, she decided it would take too long if she went that way. Instead, she directed her attention towards the tiled roof above. She could move much more quickly and avoid detection if she could get on top.

Calling Soulshadow to her hands, she spun it a few times to gain momentum and tossed it over the roof's peak, where it hooked on the side of a chimney. Tempest climbed up the cold metal chain onto the roof and, with a flick of her wrist, released the hook and called Soulshadow back to her hand.

Her sandals quietly padded on the tiles as she ran across the rooftop. Tempest leapt from one section of roof to the next and used Soulshadow when she needed to bridge a gap too large to jump across.

She stopped as she came to the end of the palace. There was a large gap between her and the somewhat shorter castle wall. Luckily, there were no guards in sight, and Tempest sent Soulshadow to the top of the wall below her. She jumped from the roof and allowed the chain to shrink as she dropped. Her feet hit the wall with a thud a few feet below the top.

Tempest leaned back and walked along the wall as the chain continued pulling her up the wall. She flung one leg over the top, repositioned Soulshadow, and quickly dropped to the street below.

Following the pull towards Aiden, Tempest darted toward the nearest alley and let her power push her faster than any mortal could run. A small amount of relief trickled through her as she sensed the distance closing between them.

She stuck to back alleys to avoid any lingering in the main streets. While she didn't fear mortals, she didn't want them to slow her down as she raced through town. After one last turn, she skidded to a stop, kicking up a cloud of dust that surrounded her. He was here.

The way was blocked by a dozen masked individuals dressed in anonymous black, each of them armed.

"*What have you done with Emperor Aiden?*" Tempest growled, letting every syllable drip with her power. To her surprise, none of the individuals appeared phased by it in any way.

"Leave now, goddess. You have no power over us," one of them replied.

Tempest's eyes widened, then narrowed to slits. "*How do you know who I am?*"

Another individual spun a dagger in their hand and laughed. "You really think your antics have gone unnoticed? You literally announced yourself in front of all of the gods only a few days ago."

Her mind raced. They must have been sent by one of the gods. But which one? And why would a god want a mortal emperor dead?

"*Hand over the emperor and I will spare you.*"

"You think we fear you? You are a weak god. He is long gone."

Tempest scoured the group in front of her, verifying the claim. Aiden wasn't with them. But she could feel him. He was either nearby or Fate was messing with her. She swore she would find out who Fate was if it was the latter and make them pay.

Without the need to avoid harming Aiden or hide her identity, Tempest released the bonds on her power and set Soulshadow free. It wrapped around the neck of one of the masked men and hooked into the shoulder of the one behind him. She pulled and slammed both of them into the wall, where they crumpled, unconscious.

She summoned Soulshadow back, the chain slipping through her fingers, and kept it spinning between her and the now-rushing group. With a yell, two darted to her left while another two skirted around Soulshadow to her right.

Soulshadow arced to her right and slammed into the two men as Tempest jumped over the larger part of the group. It ripped into their chests as she called it back again. The men screamed and dropped to the ground as blood stained the street.

"*You think you can win against a god? You are nothing!*"

A colorless light blinded Tempest. The arm that was spinning Soulshadow faltered as a blade sliced into her shoulder and back.

She cried out in pain and rage. Whatever god was behind this had given the mortals a blade made from cresten iron, one of the only things that could harm a god.

While she wasn't the most powerful god, she had ways to use her ability the other gods didn't know of. The bright light never dimmed, but the darkness in the souls of her attackers allowed her to locate those who now surrounded her.

She focused on their movement and noted the soul of one of the men she had sliced through fade away. Another soul darted towards her, and she swung Soulshadow. Her back protested, but she couldn't worry about that now. It connected with the man with a thud, and the soul dissipated.

Tempest kept count of the souls around her. Four had gone, and one lay still where she'd left it. Only seven left. She attempted to determine who was giving off the bright light but couldn't discern the direction it was coming from. She only knew it had utterly blinded her and was probably also a gift from their god.

Soulshadow hung from her hand, waiting to be called into action. She noticed three souls waver, becoming darker, and dropped to her knees as they moved towards her. Two of them collided with each other above her, their blades digging into the gut of the other. Their souls flickered out as they dropped on top of her.

She pushed their bodies off and swung Soulshadow upward into the jaw of the third individual. There was a loud crack. The soul dissipated immediately.

Tempest noticed a gap in the souls and crawled towards it, hoping the light was blinding everyone and not only her. Her hopes were dashed as two of the remaining four souls moved towards her, closing the gap. Her hand slipped in a pool of blood and her face smacked the ground. The four darted towards her, and she rolled onto her back to dodge them.

One attacker adjusted their direction and stomped on her stomach. Before she could register the full amount of pain, another foot came down on her shoulder, grinding her wound into the ground. Her vision darkened, and tears rimmed her eyes.

Feet kicked her from every direction until finally, someone grabbed a fist full of her hair and pulled her to her knees. Tempest could feel the cold chill of a cresten iron blade at her throat.

"Any last words, goddess of the broken?" a feminine voice mocked.

Tempest hated using certain aspects of her powers. Some of them physically hurt her to use, but she wasn't above doing it when she needed to. It appeared this was one of those moments.

"*Tell your god you failed*," Tempest spat, blood spraying from her mouth.

She called to the souls surrounding her and drew them to her. The goddess of the broken was a god of judgment, and she found these souls to be lacking.

The soul of the man Soulshadow had maimed dissipated immediately, while the other four were pulled from the flesh and blood of their hosts. Screams of agony were cut off as they snapped out of their bony prisons and were crushed within her power.

The light dissipated, and Tempest watched the four bodies drop around her through spots in her vision as it acclimated.

As tempting as laying down and resting were at the moment, she had to find Aiden. She could feel that he was close—and not alone. Two very dark souls were with him in the building to her left.

Tempest slowly rose from her knees to her feet. Each step sent a jolt of pain through her body. She focused on it to keep her going and used it to push closer to where she needed to be. Soulshadow hung from her shoulders, its chain wrapped around her torso and its spiked head leaving a trail as it was dragged through the blood on the ground.

She gripped Soulshadow's chain in her right hand as she reached the door, leaving the slack on her left side still hanging. Gathering her strength, she slammed her body into the door and burst in, ready to attack.

Tempest wasn't sure how much longer her body would last, so she immediately sent Soulshadow towards its first target. It slammed into the man's chest, and he dropped to the floor. She stretched out her other hand and called for the soul of the last assailant and pulled it from the person, crushing it as she had the others.

Pain shot behind her eyes as the soul disappeared. She sagged against the doorframe, her eyes connecting with Aiden's terrified gaze. With his hands and feet tied and a gag over his mouth, he tried to push himself away from her, only to collapse against the wall with a painfilled groan.

She peeled her body from the frame and stumbled across the room. The fear and pain radiating from Aiden through their connection turned her stomach. Releasing Soulshadow, she staggered a few steps with the disappearance of its weight. Tempest sunk down the wall beside Aiden, leaving a trail of blood on it.

"I'm not going to hurt you." Tempest groaned as she settled next to him. She lifted her hands to the gag on his mouth and untied it.

Eyes wide, Aiden shifted into a better position against the wall with a wince. "It wasn't a dream," he whispered.

Untying the straps from his hands and feet, she asked, "What wasn't?"

"In the alley. There were flashes… of you, with chains, attacking the men who had me. They beat me, and I blacked out. I thought I had made it up."

Resting her head on the wall, Tempest tried to let her body relax. "That was me."

The two sat in silence for a few minutes before Aiden spoke again. "You're actually her, aren't you?"

"Who?"

"Tempest."

"I already told you my name is Tempest."

Aiden rolled his head to face her. "You know that's not what I mean. You're a god, aren't you." It wasn't a question. He was stating it as fact.

Tempest kept her gaze on the floor in front of her. "Yeah. I am."

"Why did you help me?"

"Which time?"

"Let's start with when you healed me in the desert."

"I really didn't mean to do that. I don't regret it, but I wasn't looking for you, either."

"How did you find me, then?"

"Fate."

He huffed. "That's not an answer."

Tempest fidgeted with her fingers as she wondered how much she should tell him. "How much do you know about me? I mean, the goddess version of me?"

He rolled his head back to look at the room and sighed. "Not much. Other gods, you hear rumors of their lives from time to time; battles and arguments. Most of it, I'm sure, is completely made up. But you... you are quiet. I know you help people. I know you can judge a soul and decide what kind of person they are. You're the only god who can do that besides the ruler of Toph. You're not as powerful as the god of the dead, but you are known to be more forgiving. Of course, I just saw you rip the soul out of a man, so I'm not so sure how true that last part is."

Tempest's head snapped towards Aiden. "You saw *what?*"

"The black mist that came out of him," Aiden pointed to the body to his right, "that was his soul, right?"

Tempest's mind leapt from repose to riotous. No mortal should be able to see that. None of this made sense. Why was a god messing with an emperor? Literally taking over his body and then wiping his memory of it, but leaving this latent sense behind. Who could do that?

No, not one god. At least two. One who seized control of Aiden's body but didn't seem to want him dead, and one who was trying to end him.

Tempest's vision started to darken. Her wound wasn't closing as quickly as usual, and she was still losing blood. Cursed cresten iron.

"Yeah, that was his soul."

"Okay, anything else I need to know?"

She considered keeping the rest secret but decided otherwise. Maybe if she weren't trying to figure all of this out alone, she could actually save Aiden from whoever was trying to kill him.

"I found you in the desert because I could sense you. I can feel anyone's soul if I focus on them and am close enough, but for some reason, I could feel yours long before I found you."

"So you followed it?"

She nodded. Pain from the wound on her shoulder shot through her neck in response to the movement, and her vision tunneled for a moment. Aiden didn't notice the waver in her body when it hit.

"Would you have stumbled on me if you didn't feel my soul?"

"No."

"Wow. You weren't kidding when you said it was Fate that brought us together."

"I'm pretty sure Fate is also why I was able to heal you. That's not something I can normally do."

"You weren't lying about that either, huh? I thought you were when you told me you couldn't heal me before."

Tempest chuckled and closed her eyes as a wave of nausea hit her. "I don't make it a habit to lie very often."

"I suppose not."

It was becoming difficult to keep her body upright. She leaned her shoulder against Aiden.

He glanced over. "Are you all right?"

She shook her head. Aiden took stock and noticed the blood on the wall behind her.

"You didn't tell me you were hurt!"

He gently pushed her off of him and stood up, his body trembling with the exertion.

Tempest cracked her eyes open. "You shouldn't move, either. Someone will find us when they find the bodies I left outside."

"I'm not staying in a room with two dead bodies in it, and you aren't up to moving them."

She closed her eyes. "True."

Tempest listened as he dragged the bodies into the street and closed the door before joining her against the wall again.

"Is there more?" Aiden asked.

"More what?"

"More than I need to know."

"Are you sure you can handle it?"

He snorted. "I'm the emperor. It's my job to take care of an entire kingdom, and you are asking me if I can handle a little bit of information?"

"Something is... off about how I feel your soul. I always feel it, no matter where you are. That's not normal. It's how I found you tonight. I am in physical pain if you get too far away from me, and sometimes I can feel your emotions or your wellbeing through it, but not usually."

"You're joking, right?"

"Nope. I also think a god is trying to kill you. I don't know why, though."

"What makes you think that?"

"Those attackers tonight used blades that are deadly to gods. No mortal can make them, and no mortal should have them." Tempest breathed out through her mouth as another wave of nausea passed over her. "There's more, but I can't think straight right now."

"Do you think they expected you to track me down?"

"Well, I did threaten anyone trying to harm you, so..."

Aiden laughed. "You were quite the beautiful, bloody force to be reckoned with at the claiming ceremony, weren't you?"

Tempest could feel her strength disappearing quickly and wasn't sure how much longer it would last.

"Beautiful?" she mumbled.

"In an epic and awe-inspiring sort of way," he quickly added.

She slumped against Aiden's side and leaned her head on his shoulder. "Of course."

Aiden brushed a lock of hair from her face and looked down on her with concern. "Are you sure you're all right?"

"I'll be fine."

"Do you need me to take care of your wound?"

"No, it'll heal on its own. Nothing serious was hit. It's just going to take a long time. Are you all right?"

"Yeah. They didn't hurt me much. I'm still recovering from when they found us during your trial, but no new major injuries. I will be fine. It's crazy..."

"What is?" Tempest prompted when he didn't continue.

"It's just, I have no clue how I was injured. I remember being up on the wall watching what I could of the trial, and the next thing I knew, I was beside you outside the wall in incredible pain. I blacked out soon after. Do you remember what happened?"

Tempest considered telling him about the god using him, but was afraid of how he would take it. She'd wait until she knew more.

"No. I don't remember."

Tempest slumped against Aiden. Her head was spinning and her body felt completely drained of strength. She tried to lift herself off of him, realizing he also needed healing and therefore shouldn't be used as a support, but Aiden placed his hand on her head and laid it back on his shoulder.

"You don't need to move. We can lean on each other as we wait it out." Aiden's voice was soft. He laid his head on top of hers. "Are you sure there is nothing more I can do to help you? You've continuously saved my life, and I've done nothing in return."

She took a deep breath, powering through another wave of nausea as she prepared to answer. "There's nothing. I appreciate you asking, though. Please, don't be offended if I suddenly nod off. I'm really not feeling well."

Aiden held the back of his hand to her forehead. "You're burning up! Were you ailing still when you came to find me?"

"No. I had healed. This is from the cresten iron. It poisons the wound. If injured too badly, it can kill even a god."

"But you said you weren't seriously wounded."

"Exactly. That's why you don't need to worry about me. I'll heal."

Aiden huffed, but didn't argue. After all, only a fool would argue with a god.

The two sat in companionable silence in the dark room, Tempest fading in and out of consciousness while Aiden kept watch. Her head slid down his shoulder, causing both of their heads to bump into the wall every time she caught herself. Her head eventually slid off his shoulder entirely. Tempest cried out from the sudden pull of the movement on her wound and Aiden's head landing on her back.

"Tempest, lay down."

She mumbled something in return, but she didn't even know what, her brain was so foggy. Aiden gently helped her shift until her head lay in his lap.

"Thanks," Tempest whispered as she faded out.

"You're welcome."

CHAPTER 17

"Emperor Aiden! It's you!"

The guard's voice pulled Tempest out of her slumber. She hissed as her back protested when she moved.

"Send for a carriage to bring us back to the palace. Neither of us can handle a long walk," Aiden ordered.

Tempest slowly sat up, gently shifting her back and shoulder to see how much the wound had healed. Her eyes welled up with tears, but it was still considerably less painful than it had been before.

"How are you feeling?"

She wiped the tears from her eyes and forced a smile. "Better. You?"

"I wouldn't say better, but I don't feel any worse. Not all of us have a god's healing powers."

"Can we keep that between us? While the gods know I'm here, I think letting everyone know that I am a god will only make things more difficult."

"Agreed." Aiden groaned as he rose to his unsteady feet.

"I'm going to take a look out there while we wait for them to pick us up, see if there's anything about our attackers that I didn't notice before."

He jumped forward to catch Tempest as she struggled to get to her feet, pulling her to his chest and stumbling to keep his own balance.

"Tempest, you don't have to come. You should rest here."

She could hear the concern in his voice, and deep down, she wanted nothing more than to collapse back to the ground. He was right, though; there may have been things she missed and needed to discover for herself before evidence had a chance to be lost.

She gripped his arms as she straightened herself up. "Let me join you outside, and I will rest there."

He nodded in agreement and moved aside as Tempest took her first step towards the door. Her feet dragged on the floor; she didn't have the strength to try and lift them higher. She slowly made her way, with Aiden by her side, into the alley and deposited herself on a crate next to the door.

Several soldiers moved among the bodies in the alley while more of them stood on either side of the alley, keeping the quickly growing crowds at bay. The masks were being pulled off the attackers' faces one at a time, revealing men and women she didn't recognize. Nothing appeared extraordinary.

Aiden's voice made her jump as he asked one of the soldiers, ""Did you find any weapons?"

"No, your majesty."

"Really? They had..." Tempest stopped as a familiar bronze-skinned face was revealed. "It can't be."

"Miss?"

"Put the mask back on that woman," Aiden commanded quickly, then added more quietly, "That's one of the contestants of the Dei Electi."

The soldier quickly placed the mask back on the woman. What Tempest saw wasn't a trick of her mind, then.

Alina, representative of the goddess of the sun, had been part of the attack.

The more Tempest thought about it, the more it made sense. Soleil could impart her abilities to her representative since she was her chosen one. The Dei Electi created a connection between god and participant that would bless the mortal for rest of their life if they stayed in their god's favor. Soleil's power over pure light, worked by Alina, was what had blinded her during the attack.

"Can you hand me one of the masks?" Tempest asked the guard closest to her.

She turned it over in her hands once he retrieved it. The mask itself was simple, an expressionless face carved of wood and painted black. Only a faint pattern was etched across the inside of the mask and a thin blue stripe ran down the ties on either side of it.

The goddess of the sun sponsoring the attacks on the emperor didn't entirely make sense, though. While Tempest knew her to be prideful and jealous, she was also a very insecure god. Tempest had often helped Soleil when she was feeling redundant or lesser than the other gods, especially Kirata, goddess of the heavens. Tempest suspected that another god had manipulated Soleil's involvement. The only question was who.

"Tempest," Sylvia said quietly, "I'm sorry."

Tempest looked at her. "For what?"

"For what they're saying about you."

Tempest's face darkened. She looked out into the courtyard that connected their rooms. They'd spent the last hour enjoying each other's company in Tempest's room.

"What are they saying?"

"That you killed Alina. Well, only half of them are saying that. The rest decided that you were sleeping with Emperor Aiden."

Tempest's eyes blazed. "They're lying."

"I know," Sylvia said soothingly, "but it's hard to prove."

Tempest looked at Sylvia with wide eyes. "I wasn't sleeping with him!"

"I know," Sylvia said again. "I believe you."

Tempest looked at Sylvia as her emotions warred in her heart. It had been so long since she'd had a friend. For the first time in over a century, she wished she could have someone in whom she could be open with, completely honest about everything. The more she thought about it, the more she realized that she had never really had that before.

"I wish I could leave," she whispered. "Just get out of here. Be anywhere but here."

Sylvia frowned. "You've got a chance to be a leader of the country. You've got to take that chance."

Tempest looked at her and shook her head. "You know, just because a god chooses you to compete in the Dei Electi doesn't mean you have to become empress. Representatives can say no at any point."

"But why would you want to? You could do something good for the people."

"There are other ways."

"Are you really going to leave?"

Tempest felt along her connection to Aiden. It unsettled her that it was becoming a comforting action for her.

"No. I have too much to do."

Sylvia looked confused but chose not to push it. A knock sounded on the door had immediately brought Sylvia her feet. She opened the door, but no one was there. Only a letter lay on the floor. She picked it up and brought it to Tempest, who opened it.

Dei Electi Contestant,

An empress must be wise, just, and brave.

The next trial will commence tomorrow. Meet in the ballroom at midday. Only contestants will be admitted.

Tempest read the missive twice and passed it to Sylvia.

"What do you think it means?" Sylvia asked.

"They're judging our character. Any guesses on who will fail and be sent home?" Tempest asked with a wry grin.

Sylvia smirked and leaned back in her chair. "There are a few that I hope are part of that crowd."

Tempest approached the ballroom the next afternoon and stopped short. The other contestants had dressed up, many wearing elaborate clothing and ornate jewelry. But Tempest felt confident in her simple red gown. She wasn't interested in standing out any more than she already had. Besides, after all she'd been through lately, she deserved the comfort of doing without all that finery. Her shoulder was healing, though at a mortal's pace, and certain movements were still painful.

The double doors opened, and the women were ushered in. A man stood at the head of the room, a table with stacks of various quills, ink, and paper in front of him. More tables and chairs were arranged around the ballroom.

"Welcome, contestants." The man's voice echoed in the grand hall. "Please select your writing implements and find a seat."

The women silently made their way towards the table. Tempest found the variety of writing tools intriguing. Quills from an array of birds were spread out on the table. Most of the representatives quickly grabbed the finest quality items—golden peacock quills, silky parchment, and ink in jeweled bottles.

While they were beautiful, Tempest knew that no matter the cost of the tools used in this contest, it wouldn't help them with their answers. She chose a crow quill, papyrus scroll, and a simple glass bottle of black ink and made her way to a table in the back of the room.

She sat down and took a breath. The room was full of competitors, strangers; potentially enemies, as well. To calm her mind, she breathed deeply, rhythmically. The scent of patchouli assaulted her nostrils.

A servant moved from table to table, placing a piece of parchment paper face down on their tables. The man at the head of the room moved in front of the table and crossed his arms.

"In front of you, you will find a problem, one that you will be expected to present a solution to within the next hour. When you are finished, bring it up to me along with the items you used. The emperor and his advisors will review your responses. Those deemed good enough will be given the opportunity to spend time individually with the emperor. The rest will be asked to leave. You may begin."

Tempest flipped the paper over and read the problem. Just as she suspected; a generic situation about how to handle a drought as a ruler. Dipping her quill in the ink, she began writing her solution.

A few minutes passed before the other women started to look at Tempest. She tried to put them from her mind, but she could feel their stares. Then she heard the whispers. Some about her dress, others about her hair, but the majority were about her and the emperor.

Tempest was used to the rumors and whispers. She'd experienced it all of her existence. But being in the room of women, all of whom were staring at her, was uncomfortable. She felt like she was out of place. She wanted to stand up and leave, but she kept writing.

Perhaps if she ignored them, they would leave her alone.

Tempest wrote quickly, the ink flowing onto the page. She could feel the words coming out of her heart and running onto the page like a river. It was a beautiful feeling, that she didn't have to *try* to write because she couldn't *stop* writing. It felt good to let herself get lost in the words.

When she looked up from the page, she was surprised to find that most of the women were already gone. Once her ink was dry, she rolled up her parchment, gathered her things, and brought them to the man at the front. Placing them in their own pile on the table, she quickly left.

Chapter 18

A man in fine robes stopped her as soon as she stepped into the hallway.

"Tempest, representative of the goddess of the broken. Please, follow me."

"Am I not done?"

He shook his head. "That was only the beginning. We have prepared a meal with several esteemed guests."

While Tempest didn't mind the change, she was sure that several of the competitors would not be so indifferent, especially without their escorts.

She followed him to a courtyard near the ballroom. A large fountain sat at the center, a carved sphynx standing with wings outstretched. Its eyes were closed, though its lips were parted slightly as if singing, the water spewing from its mouth to a pool at its feet. The feet rested on the edge of the pool, each carved into a different creature: a horse, a lion, an eagle, and lastly, a bull.

Tables with chairs were spread throughout the courtyard with flickering candles in mosaic lanterns at their center. A mixture of jasmine and mint was in the air, an aroma that sank bone-deep and left a sense of relaxation in its wake.

Tempest followed the man through the surprisingly crowded courtyard to a long table. Emperor Aiden sat at the middle with several guests of honor on either side of him. The man gestured to Aiden, and Tempest approached. She bowed as the man announced her.

"I see you've finished the exam," Aiden stated rigidly.

Tempest rose. "I did. Such a simple task you gave us, don't you think? It's almost as if there was more to it than the question itself."

A young man sitting at Aiden's right laughed. "You weren't kidding, Aiden. She is a feisty one."

She took a moment and focused her attention on the young man. Something about him was familiar, but she couldn't put her finger on it. His face was bright, his hair light brown, and his eyes a piercing blue. He'd dressed in a knee-length tunic with gold trim around the collar. His smile was friendly enough, but his eyes were distant, as if there were thoughts in his head that made him sad.

"Don't go spilling my secrets, Aeon. Not all of our contestants are as they seem," Aiden said with a smirk.

Tempest could feel a blush growing and told herself to stop. He was mortal. Nothing could ever come of anything between them other than heartbreak.

Her heart must have been tampered with by whatever Fate had done to her. She looked at her hands for a moment before looking up with a perfect smile.

"Now, don't go spilling *my* secrets, Emperor."

Aiden acquiesced with a nod and motioned to the people sitting near him. "Tempest, meet my cousin Aeon. Beside him are his parents, Grand Duchess Firina and Duke Bok."

The older couple smiled and nodded at her, to which Tempest responded in kind.

Aiden gestured towards his other side and continued, "These are my grandmothers, Dowager Empress Marigal and Princess Trudin."

The dowager empress gave her a warm smile. The princess looked Tempest over with apparent disgust, her white hair a stark contrast to her golden skin. Neither looked old enough to be grandmothers, but Tempest assumed that's what money and connections could get a woman.

Tempest bowed to the table once again. "It's a pleasure to meet you." Her eyes connected with Aiden's as she rose, and a feeling of safety surged through their connection.

The man who'd escorted her cleared his throat to get her attention and motioned for her to move along. She sent Aiden a small smile and left to join the crowd. She wandered around after her escort abandoned her, trying to avoid the glares and distrustful looks many of the attendees wore. When someone courageously spat in her direction, a small hand grabbed her arm and pulled her out of the way before it could hit her.

"Will you all stop? This is no way to treat a god's representative unless you are prepared to face their wrath!"

Tempest turned to see who her protector was and was relieved that Sylvia had found her. The two hurried away from the grumbling group and escaped to a table near the courtyard wall.

"Are you all right?" Sylvia asked once they were seated.

"I'm fine, thank you. When did you get so brave?"

Sylvia raised a brow and scoffed. "Brave? No! I'm just pissed off. I hate the gossip of things that people know nothing about."

A waiter approached and placed two glasses of wine on the table, for which the women thanked him. They both reached for the refreshment and took a sip. It was sweet, and yet there was something bitter about it. Tempest rarely drank alcohol anyway, and wrote the odd taste off as her lack of experience.

"I'm glad I have you in my corner, Sylvia. I definitely would never want to be on the other end of your wrath."

"Oh, you have no idea," Sylvia replied with a wiggle of her brows.

The two laughed, and Tempest turned her focus on the crowd around them.

"Did you meet Aeon?" Sylvia asked.

"I did. He seems a decent man."

"He's the next in line, you know. If Aiden doesn't produce an heir."

"Really? I didn't know, but it would make sense that he would be here, then."

Tempest tried to think about what she knew of the current royal family. After the first few decades of living among the mortals and avoiding the noble circles, she'd lost track of the political drama and ties within the kingdom. She realized now that she really didn't know much.

Sylvia took another sip. "I wouldn't mind marrying him instead."

Intrigued, Tempest returned her gaze to find her friend blushing.

"Really? Why's that?"

"I've been in the palace since I was a girl and first met him when he was a youth as well. He has never treated a servant as below him. Sure, he asks us for stuff, but that's our job. He's always respectful, though."

"Sounds like he would make a decent emperor."

Sylvia waved her glass in front of her, sloshing some of the wine on her maroon dress. "I don't mean that Emperor Aiden isn't a good emperor. He does a fine job."

Tempest took in the state of her friend and surreptitiously sniffed her own drink. The chances of getting drunk were minimal for herself, but she hadn't expected Sylvia to become this tipsy so quickly. She'd only had one glass of wine, but her face was red, and she wavered a little in her chair. Had the mortals changed how they fermented alcohol recently? Or had Sylvia been imbibing before she caught up to Tempest?

"I never thought you considered otherwise," Tempest replied with a warm smile, keeping her voice soft and comforting.

She returned her attention to the guests and noted that many of the contestants also looked unsteady. The crowd parted for a moment, and Tempest saw Aiden leaving his chair, his hand locked with the god of love's representative, Faith.

She tapped into her connection with Aiden and was shocked when she detected lust. Her fist clenched, and the glass she was holding shattered, scattering wine and debris all over the table. Aiden wasn't hers, and never could be, but someone was going to pay, be it Fate, whoever they were, or Amias, Faith's godly sponsor. Something was amiss, and Tempest refused to sit idly by and watch it happen.

The crowd shifted again, and Tempest lost sight of Aiden and Faith.

"Sylvia, stay here for a moment. I need to run and grab something. I'll be right back."

Before Sylvia could reply, Tempest was already up and hastening towards where she had last seen Aiden. She grew angrier every time she tapped into her connection with him, and only did so momentarily to figure out which way to go. While she couldn't completely tune it out, she did allow her anger to override her emotions and help block the sensations.

She made her way through a large metal gate and entered another courtyard, this one much smaller than the one she'd just left. A moan from the other side drew her attention, and she immediately saw red—literally, saw red. Her goddess ability surged forward and revealed an unnatural red aura surrounding Aiden and Faith.

Fists clenched, Tempest stormed over to the two and tore them apart.

"How dare you!"

"We're a little busy, Tempest. Why don't you wait your turn over..." Aiden stopped talking when Tempest's fist came in contact with his face.

"You shush and wait *your* turn!"

Tempest turned on Faith. She wanted to smack the smirk right off the woman's beautiful face like she had with Aiden, but since she had less history with Faith, she refrained.

"I know what you are doing, and you will not get away with it."

Faith shrugged and pasted on a coy smile. "I don't know what you're talking about. It appears it isn't just you the emperor is interested in. I wonder if he would go for any woman willing to entertain him? Should we see?"

Aiden had recovered and tried to move past Tempest, but she gripped his arm and held him back.

"Whatever Amias told you or gave you, ask yourself if it's worth it. Do you really want to be with someone who doesn't actually love you? You can still win the emperor's heart without cheating."

"I don't know what you're talking about."

"Come on, Faith, we both know better."

When she didn't get a response, Tempest called on her ability to sense Faith's soul. The crushing, broken heartbeat she found surprised her.

"Faith, did you have someone you already loved? Before you came here?"

Faith's eyes darted away and her smirk faltered. "There was no one."

Aiden squirmed in Tempest's grip. "Let me go, Tempest. I command you as your emperor!"

She shot him a glare that left him cowering. Faith watched the interaction with interest.

Tempest returned her attention to Faith. "How about we agree not to lie to one another, Faith."

"It doesn't matter what my past is," Faith huffed. "I am here as a contestant of Dei Electi."

Tempest's anger towards Faith began to ebb as she felt the woman's soul crack a little more.

"It does matter," she encouraged, putting a little of her godly power in her voice. "A god can't force you to participate if you are chosen. Amias could have chosen another. Only one contestant will win, anyway. You can always go back to whoever you left behind."

Faith looked stricken, and a tear rolled down her face.

"I can't. Amias won't let me. They took away his love for me."

Aiden yelped as Tempest inadvertently squeezed his arm. She let go and shrugged a quiet apology. He shot her a dirty look as he rubbed his arm.

"The gods are *not* supposed to interfere like that. I am willing to help you if you don't want this."

Faith eyed her warily. "How can you help me?"

Tempest contemplated her next words. While she was sure Amias knew she was here, she didn't want the other mortals to realize she was a god.

"I am the representative of the goddess of the broken. She thinks she can help undo whatever Amias has done."

"Really?" Faith whispered. Tears streamed down her face freely now.

Tempest nodded. "She does. You need to help her first by telling me what you did to Aiden and the other contestants."

Faith withdrew a small red vial from a pocket in her gown. "Amias left me this. I was told to put it in the emperor's drink and lead him here, that I would be chosen, and Amias would bless my family for following his guidance."

"What about the other girls?"

Faith shook her head, bewildered. "I didn't do anything to them."

Tempest decided to wait until later to unravel that mystery and took the vial from Faith. "I understand. Rejoin the party and consider what it is you really want. If you wish to be with the one you love, return home and give the goddess of the broken a bit of time. Be patient. She will help you; you have her word."

Faith wiped the tears from her eyes, thanked Tempest, and left the small courtyard.

Aiden took a step to follow her before Tempest grabbed his arm once again. "Oh, no you don't. Now, what do we do with you? Stay put for a moment while I see what she gave you."

Tempest took the stopper off and sniffed the bottle. It was definitely a love potion, but she couldn't quite tell which one. She wouldn't be surprised if Amias had created some new ones while she'd been among the mortals. Without knowing which potion it was, however, she couldn't find the antidote, leaving her with only one option—to eradicate it from his body with her power.

Tucking the vial in her pocket, she took a deep breath, pulled a pouting Aiden to her, popped herself up on her tiptoes, and connected his lips with hers. Aiden struggled to push away from her for a moment, then melted into her. His arms wrapped around her waist, and he lifted her up, pulling her flat against his chest.

Well, at least it was working. But what Tempest had intended to be a short kiss quickly became anything but that. She knew she should pull away. If he was this responsive to her still, the potion had to have been burned away with her energy. She didn't want to end it, though. Tempest wrapped her arms around his neck and let the fingers of one hand slip into his hair.

Aiden moaned as he turned them until she was between him and the wall. The pressure only intensified her desire, and their kiss deepened.

She was panting when he pulled his face away from hers and looked her in the eye. A warm smile that reached his eyes spread across his face as he spoke. "I've missed this, Tempest. We've got to quit meeting like this."

Tempest shoved him away. This wasn't Aiden. Not anymore. The god was back. She knew who it was this time, and wasn't sure she liked it.

Chapter 19

"You! How dare you use a mortal's body!" Tempest slipped away from the wall to give herself room to flee if needed.

Aiden took a step forward, arms outstretched, and she took a step back.

"Please let me explain, Tempest. It's not what you think!"

"It's against the rules to use a mortal's body. You may be the god of the dead, but that does not give you the right to do whatever you please."

She mentally kicked herself for not making the connection sooner. Aiden's current name was only a slight variation of the one he typically used.

He sighed. "It's not like that! Will you just listen? I don't have much time. I don't know why I can speak to you, but it shouldn't be possible."

"Why not?"

"This is my trial."

She swallowed. "This... this is your mortal trial?"

Aiden nodded. "It is. My godly consciousness should be locked away until it's over, but something happened when I met you. You know our memories are erased when we're born into a mortal body and a spell is cast so other gods can't recognize us. Maybe Vesper messed up, or—"

"Wait, what does Vesper have to do with this?"

"You don't know? Of course not. You've been gone so long you wouldn't know. He took over the mortal trials. He's now the one who plans what will happen. We go to him and tell him the level we want to ascend to, and he sets up the mortal trial with, well, for lack of a better word, trials to reach that point. If we fail here, we don't get to ascend."

Tempest's mind raced with the implications. Vesper was the god of stars and time. Sylvia was his representative. If he chose her for Aiden's Dei Electi, did that mean Vesper had chosen her for him?

"You rarely do mortal trials. Why now?"

Aiden ran a hand across his face. "Something has the dead uneasy. I went to Vesper in secret to try and ascend several levels at once. The other gods don't know I'm gone. I haven't trusted them since they drove you out of the land of the gods."

Tempest ran a hand through her hair as she processed what he was saying. Maybe Vesper had intentionally made her find him. She just didn't understand why.

"How many mortal souls do you have behind your power right now?" she asked.

"Four."

Her jaw dropped. “That’s it? I know being god of the dead makes you much more powerful than most gods with just your own soul, but those other gods usually have at least ten!”

“Which would be why I snuck away to do one now! I’m not strong enough to take on multiple gods on my own.”

“You have Vesper.”

Aiden rolled his eyes. “He’s been busy.”

Tempest crossed her arms. “Doing what?”

“It’s not my place to tell,” Aiden said, shaking his head. “All I can say is that several of the gods have been doing mortal trials. They’ve built up large reserves to draw power from. I can’t compete with that.”

A pang of guilt hit Tempest. Aiden and Vesper were the only two gods who hadn’t used her when she was there. While the rest manipulated her into solving their petty fights, they never did. She hadn’t said goodbye or told them that she was leaving.

“Are you mad?” Tempest whispered.

He didn’t ask what she meant. “I was at first, but not anymore. I understand what your life was like there.” Aiden shifted his body weight and looked at the ground. “Are you happy?”

Tempest was tempted to approach him but stayed where she was instead. “Somewhat. I don’t regret leaving. It gets lonely, though.”

Aiden nodded and looked into her eyes. “Are you coming back?”

"I don't know." Her heart broke as his face dropped. "I do know that I will help you, though. Maybe Vesper planned for us to meet during your trial. Even a god isn't immune to the tampering of a mortal life."

He gave her a sad smile. "Thank you."

"You're welcome."

"So, that kiss..." a smirk spread across Aiden's face.

Tempest gave him a playful shove and rolled her eyes. "Don't even start. Do you have any idea when your mortal self will be back?"

Aiden shook his head and shrugged.

"Do you remember anything about your mortal life?"

"I remember all of it."

Tempest started walking towards the gate. "Let's get you back to your party, then, before you're missed and I get blamed for it. Maybe you can clear things up a bit; you know, help make everyone in your palace a bit less hostile towards me. I'll come up with an excuse for your mortal side, since he won't remember any of it."

Aiden followed closely behind. "This is weird."

She laughed. "You're telling me."

The two parted ways as soon as they walked through the gate, Aiden making his way back to his seat and Tempest back to a very drunk-looking Sylvia.

"How much did you drink?" Tempest asked her now-hiccupping friend.

"Just this one, I swear." Sylvia repeated the last word a few times, emphasizing different words with each pass.

Tempest sat at the table and snatched the half-empty glass from Sylvia's hand. She focused on it and found it glowed a sickeningly green hue. Tempest hadn't expected her sight to work, but occasionally the residual intent of someone would be left on an item, and Tempest could use that to help judge a soul. The residue matched the soul it came from, and she was very familiar with this one.

She quickly glanced through the crowd and easily found Isabella, the representative of Aloysius, the god of war, sitting at a table with other contestants. If she didn't have a similar green hue around her soul, she would still have been one of Tempest's suspects. She was also the only one who looked even slightly sober in the group.

Sylvia tried to stand and stumbled. Tempest caught her, stopping her from smacking her chin in the corner of the table, and helped her back to her feet.

Deciding to wait until later to confront Isabella, she helped Sylvia back to her room. If the worst of it was everyone getting drunk, then so be it. But something irritated Tempest. Isabella seemed awfully comfortable with everyone else being tipsy around her. Something just didn't add up right.

She laid Sylvia on her bed and pulled the covers over her before heading back to her own room.

Though the sun was still high, Tempest was exhausted. Her injury was still healing, she'd written an extensive essay as part of Dei Electi, survived snubs from snobs, and discovered the god of the dead in the midst of his mortal trial. The day had already drained her completely. She slipped under her covers and quickly fell asleep.

She twisted and turned, at once both awake and asleep. In her dream, Aiden was attempting to explain his reasons for playing a mortal life, and Tempest was sitting across from him with a puzzled look and a glass of wine. They were on a patio, and above them, the stars were bright.

"Tempest, wake up. We've got a big day ahead of us."

Sylvia's voice pulled Tempest out of the dream. She had been so wrapped up in it that she hadn't even noticed that her room was no longer empty.

Tempest found Sylvia sitting on the floor in her room, a tray of fruits and cheeses in front of her. "What's going on?"

"Isabella attacked one of the contestants last night. She's been put in the dungeons until she can be punished."

The covers flew off of Tempest as she suddenly sat up. "What?! Who?"

"The god of luck's representative, Aurora. That's not even the craziest part. The sun never set last night, either. It's sitting at midday."

Tempest saw beads of sweat on Sylvia's face and realized it was several degrees hotter than it usually would be. If the sun never set, the temperature would never drop and reset for the day.

Sylvia picked the tray up, set it on the nightstand, and then sat on the edge of the bed. "There are rumors that it's the goddess in mourning for the death of her representative," she whispered, as if afraid someone would overhear her.

Tempest doubted it was done in mourning for the hapless woman. She guessed that it was instead a punishment for her death. A punishment, and a warning, for Tempest.

"You mentioned Isabella is in the dungeon. How did she attack Aurora?"

"At the party yesterday. I don't remember much of it, and neither does anyone else, really, but apparently Isabella attacked her with a dagger and tried to kill her. Emperor Aiden stopped her in time. I didn't see it, but apparently he moved extremely fast. It was incredible!"

Tempest assumed the god of the dead was still in control when that happened. How else would he have been able to move so quickly?

She quickly got out of bed and went to get changed. The only black dress she had slipped over her curves. Tempest had a feeling she would need to wear something today that could hide the color of blood.

Sylvia came over to help adjust the back so it fit correctly. “Where are you suddenly taking off to?”

“I need to find someone. I won’t be long, but it may be best to stay in your room for the day. Don’t let anyone in unless it’s me."

Sylvia nodded, eyes wide. “You think it may still be unsafe?”

“Think about it; you were black-out drunk with less than a single glass of wine. So was everyone else there yesterday. There’s got to be more going on than just a drunk woman attacking another drunk woman. I think you were drugged.”

“Oh. I didn’t think about that.” Sylvia’s fingers twitched nervously in front of her.

Tempest faced her friend and placed her hands on her shoulders. “It will all be fine. Your god seems to care a great deal about your safety, and I will figure out what is going on. Just be smart while I do this, so I don’t worry. All right?”

It took Sylvia a moment to realize what Tempest had just said. “Wait! What do you mean, my god cares about my safety? What do you know?”

Tempest regretted having said anything and, with a gentle hand on her friend’s back, ushered Sylvia back to her own room.

“Never mind, it’s not important right now. Just stay here until I get back.”

With a slight smile, Sylvia sighed in resignation and closed and locked the door, leaving Tempest alone in the hall.

Tempest used their connection to find Aiden and took off. She assumed his mortal self had taken control by now, but she needed to see him immediately and convince him to let her speak with Isabella—hopefully, without him asking too many questions.

CHAPTER 20

Tempest followed their connection until she finally found Aiden exiting a room with the prominent members of his court. She stopped to wait for him and watched from the shadows until he turned and locked eyes with her. He didn't look away as he finished his goodbyes.

Tempest's heart raced and pounded in her chest as she waited for him. Each beat vibrated her skin and made the hairs on her arms stand on end. She stepped out of the shadows and moved toward him.

"I was hoping you would come to find me today."

His smile both broke and melted her heart. She looked but only saw the mortal Aiden today. There was no sign that the god of the dead was still present.

"Can we talk for a moment? Alone?" Tempest asked.

Aiden's brow rose, an unspoken question at the tip of his tongue, but instead of asking it, he gestured for her to follow him into the room he had just exited.

The door click shut behind her as Tempest wandered into the room, trying to decide how best to broach the topic of yesterday's events. She decided to just do it and quickly turned to face him.

"What do you remember from yesterday?" she blurted.

Aiden blushed. "Uh, I remember being at the party, and seeing you. Soon after, things become a bit blurry. I left with Faith, and then you accused her of... drugging me? Then we..." his face grew even redder, and he cleared his throat before continuing, "kissed. After that, nothing, until I woke up in my bed this morning. I was just informed that I saved someone from an attack, which I don't remember, and was about to go down and speak to the woman."

Tempest stewed over his story for a moment. She hadn't been sure if he would remember that they had kissed, and based on his reaction just now, she had a feeling it had complicated things.

"May I join you?" she asked.

"You want to go see the woman in the dungeon?"

"I do. I have some questions for Isabella. There were a few odd things that happened yesterday besides the attack that I have a feeling were either connected to her or to the god she represents."

He stared at her, waiting for her to elaborate.

"I can explain more, but with or without you, I will be seeing her."

"You really want to go?"

"I really need to go."

"All right, then. I want to know everything, though."

"Deal."

Tempest explained the aura she had seen on the glass of wine, the effect it had had on those at the party, and how she had seen it around Isabella. She mentioned the difference in Isabella's sobriety level compared to the rest of the party. Combined with what they knew of the attack Aiden thwarted, the information told the whole story except one part—why?

With only one way to find that answer, they went together to the dungeon and were shown to Isabella's cell.

Tempest approached the bars, but Aiden gripped her arm, holding her back. She turned and read the silent query in his expression.

"I'm fine," Tempest reassured him. "I promise. I've seen much worse things than a woman in a cell. You have no clue how many wars and battles I've lived through."

He quickly schooled the shock from his face as Isabella laughed with a voice that wasn't at all hers.

"That you did, didn't you, goddess of the broken?" Isabella's voice was deep and her face contorted into an angry snarl.

Tempest gripped a bar and leaned in. "You shouldn't be doing this, Aloysius. You know it's against the rules."

Isabella leaned against the cell wall and picked her teeth with the bone of a small animal. Tempest wondered how she had gotten that so quickly, but chose not to dwell on it.

"Things are changing, Tempest. The rules won't matter in the same way soon. Who's going to punish me now, that you're gone?"

"There're always other gods to do the job. I'm one of the weaker ones, anyway."

A sickening laugh echoed in the stone cell. "You and I both know that's a lie. You may have the other gods fooled, but I've seen you on the battlefield. You've ruined many perfectly good wars for me."

Tempest released a dramatic sigh and leaned her forehead on the bars in exasperation. "If you didn't keep starting wars in the mortal world, I wouldn't need to step in and end them."

Isabella stood and sauntered towards the bars. She put her face right in front of Tempest's until their foreheads were pressed together.

"You didn't follow the rules, either. They thought you were a hero. You must be the richest person alive by now, with all of the offerings they gave you for your accomplishments. None of the other gods believed me when I told them it was you down on the battlefield. No, no one thought a god would stoop so low as to don mortal armor and fight alongside them. You never were afraid to stoop to low levels, though, now were you, sweet little Tempest?"

Aiden opened his mouth to speak and moved towards the cell, but Tempest held out her arm to stop him. She focused on Isabella and searched for the mortal soul within, to judge whether she could help her. The soul was dark, but not thoroughly corrupted. There was still enough for Tempest to work with.

Tempest let her power build within her before she spoke. "Aloysius, why did you make Isabella attack Aurora?"

Isabella let out a low chuckle and turned her back on Tempest, her head never leaving the bars. "I know what you're doing, Tempest. It's not going to work on me."

"Don't make me hurt the woman to get you out of her, Aloysius." Tempest pushed her power into her voice. "*God of War, leave this mortal's body if you will not answer my questions. I will force you out if I need to.*"

She watched Isabella's soul flicker as it fought against the god inhabiting her body.

"*The mortal wants you out, and I will help her regain control.*"

Isabella dug her nails into the palms of her hands and slammed her head back onto the bars, making Tempest pull back from them. "Fine! Know that I'm done, Tempest. We're waiting for you." With a wicked grin, she turned around and fixed Aiden with a look. "We're waiting for both of you."

Isabella's body went slack, and she dropped to the floor of her cell, her eyes closed and breath steady. Tempest checked to ensure her soul was alone in the body. She reassured Aiden with a nod and signaled for him to have the cell opened.

Tempest entered as soon as she was able and dropped to the ground next to Isabella. She gently touched the side of her face and repeated her name until Isabella woke up.

Isabella took in her surroundings, clearly confused, until she saw Aiden and hurried to her knees to bow. "Your majesty! I'm not..."

Aiden entered the cell and squatted down in front of her. "Isabella, we need to ask you a few questions. Are you willing to answer them?"

Isabella raised her head and noted the two guards now standing outside the cell. She nodded and looked back at the emperor.

"Tell us what you remember of yesterday."

"I remember the test, and a man outside the door who escorted me to the party and the emperor." Isabella looked up at Aiden through her lashes and smiled.

Envy made Tempest want to strip the flirtatious look off Isabella's face, especially since the woman had Aiden's undivided attention. Still, she reminded herself once again that Aiden couldn't be hers. He was a god doing a mortal trial, and she couldn't interfere.

"Anything after that?" Tempest pried.

Isabella turned towards her and shrugged. "Not much. Just bits and pieces, like a bad dream. I'm sorry."

Aiden placed his hand on Isabella's shoulder. "Your god, it seems, wanted to directly intervene with the Dei Electi." He looked at Tempest as he added, "You will not be punished for his actions."

Tempest gave a single nod of agreement and looked away from the two. Without making eye contact, she warned Isabella, "Until the contest is over, I highly suggest taking leafsbane. It will not harm you, but will help prevent your god from overstepping his bounds again. He can still aid and communicate with you, but he will not be able to take over your body again."

"He did *what?!*" Isabella roared.

Tempest was glad to see the warrior within Isabella reemerging. Knowing a little of what Aloysius did ignited a fire in the woman, and she no longer appeared weak and helpless. Tempest rose and moved toward the door to exit the cell.

"I'll allow the emperor to explain it to you. I have other things I need to attend to, if you will excuse me." Tempest sketched a quick bow and hurried to leave the dungeon.

Aiden's voice soothing Isabella followed her, and tears welled up in her eyes. Tempest knew she shouldn't feel this way—really, shouldn't feel anything for the man other than protective—but not everything about being a god was so very different from being a mortal. They loved and felt the sting of loss, as well.

As she made her way back to Sylvia's room, Tempest couldn't help questioning how those two had become so close. Her mind created scenarios where Isabella and Aiden had slipped away alone, with no one knowing. Each one made her angrier than the last.

Tempest's blood boiled and her face reddened as she walked down the hall. She shoved the door to Sylvia's room open and found it empty.

"Where is Sylvia?" she called to the guard posted at the door.

"She went with several of the other contestants. They wanted to speak with her. She'll be returned to her room shortly."

"Fine. Be here when she is." Tempest started back to her room, then changed course. "Oh, and if anyone should come looking for me, I'm out."

She didn't bother waiting for a response. It wasn't until she'd stomped off the palace grounds and was out in the city that she realized just how angry she was. Her hands were clenched so tight her knuckles had turned white, and she was gritting her teeth. It took a great deal of effort to calm herself down, but by the time she'd looped back to the palace, she'd managed to get herself under control.

When she arrived at Sylvia's room, the guard informed her that the other contestants had left not long ago and Sylvia napping. Tempest thanked him before entering the room and closing the door behind her. She stood there for a moment looking at

Sylvia's peacefully sleeping form before moving to sit in a chair beside the bed.

She stayed there for hours, just watching Sylvia sleep and thinking. What had happened in the land of the gods to cause them to run so rampant and directly disobey the rules they were all committed to? What could have occurred to make the god of the dead choose to do a mortal trial in secret?

Tempest looked outside and saw that the sun still hadn't moved. Why did the gods seem to be deteriorating?

Tempest was snapped out of her thoughts by Sylvia's sudden movement. She sat up and watched as Sylvia coughed, sweating profusely. Tempest tried to wake her up, but to no avail. She rushed to the door and told the guard to get the physician.

Sylvia's skin was hot to the touch, and her breathing was labored. Tempest did her best to cool her down with a damp cloth, but it didn't seem to be helping much.

Soon the guard returned with the physician and his apprentice, and Tempest moved out of their way.

"Do you know what happened to her?" the physician asked.

Tempest chewed on her nails as she watched him work. "No. She went out with several contestants, and when I returned, I found her sleeping. She wasn't like this at first."

The man lifted Sylvia's eyelids and tipped her head towards the light before closing them once again. "Anything off about her before that?"

"I haven't known her long, but I can't think of anything. Wait! She was sweating some this morning. Nothing like this, though. I just assumed it was from the heat."

The physician took Sylvia's wrist to check her pulse. "I'm finding more and more cases of people in this sort of state. It's only continuing to get hotter, and people are falling ill from the effects. I've lost half of my staff already from it. Until the sun goddess decides to give us peace, I don't see this going away."

Tempest's goddess powers grew harder to control as her anger grew. Her breathing grew labored as she fought to control it.

The physician's apprentice stepped forward. "We're going to have to take her to the infirmary."

As Tempest was about to offer to care for her, there was a knock at the door. Aiden's cousin, Aeon, poked his head in. He looked so different today compared to yesterday, looking somber and concerned rather than lighthearted.

"I'm sorry if I am interrupting. I heard Sylvia was ill."

Tempest watched as he entered and tentatively approached the bed.

"How is she?"

Remembering how Sylvia spoke of Aeon, Tempest took another deep breath to calm herself and replied, "She's not well. She'll need to be closely taken care of to pull through. I will—"

"I'll do it," Aiden interrupted. "I can stay with her." His shoulders were slumped, and tears rimmed his eyes.

"How well do you know Sylvia? She mentioned that you two knew each other. I hadn't realized you were so close."

"We've been friends since we were children," Aeon replied without taking his eyes off Sylvia. "As we grew older, I wasn't around as often, so we grew apart, but we've still always been friends."

Tempest had a feeling there was likely more to it, but chose not to press him. She needed to get to the root of this problem, which meant doing the last thing she wanted to.

"If you're willing to stay with her, I would appreciate it. I need to take care of something that will call me away for a while."

"Done. I have nowhere I would rather be."

The physician gave Aeon instructions on how to take care of Sylvia and when to call for him again. As he and his apprentice prepared to leave, he addressed Tempest.

"All of the contestants are being kept in the palace, even those who have been selected to leave. With the heat outside, it is not safe to travel."

She hadn't realized that the impending cuts had already been made, but now that she thought about it, that must have been what Aiden and his court were doing when she found him earlier.

"I understand." Tempest gave a quick goodbye to the physician and his assistant before turning to Aeon. "Take good care of her for me, will you? She's the only friend I've got."

He only gave her a quick glance before fixing his attention back to Sylvia. "I promise."

Deciding that would have to do, Tempest left the room in search of Aiden. As much as she didn't want to see him right now, she needed to go to the land of the gods, and with her strange connection to him, she didn't dare leave him behind.

CHAPTER 21

"How much further do we have to go?" Aiden's feet dragged through the sand as he followed Tempest.

All sense of time had disappeared long ago for the two of them. Between the scorching heat of the desert and the sun not moving, there was no way to keep track.

Aiden kicked the sand, spraying it towards Tempest. "Why aren't you answering me?! I followed you into this Soleil-forsaken desert, my skin is peeling, and you decide you aren't talking to me?!"

A hand touched his shoulder, and he jumped. When he looked, he saw Tempest behind him. He turned to look at the Tempest he'd been following and found she was gone. He stopped and hung his head.

"Are you alright?" Tempest asked softly as she turned him towards her.

"I thought I was following you," he mumbled.

"This is the eleventh time this has happened since we left. A few mirages are common and expected, but I think Soleil may be targeting you at this point."

Aiden's demeanor worried Tempest. He hadn't appeared this broken either of the times she'd saved him. She also worried that as they drew closer to the gate to the land of the gods, the spells protecting it from mortals would mess with his mind, although it usually directed them to just move around it. If Tempest could have left him at the palace, she would have. No one should be out in the desert right now; even she was starting to feel the effects of the heat. It was no wonder Aiden was, too.

Tempest unwrapped the covering over her head and put one end of it in Aiden's hand. "We're getting close. Don't let go. Hopefully, it will ease once we get to the other side."

It was clear from Aiden's wary gaze that he wasn't entirely sure he was seeing the actual Tempest.

It had taken every ounce of courage she had to find Aiden and bring him along. She cursed the excruciating pain distance would cause from the connection between the two of them. Even though he was a god in a mortal body, mortals were not supposed to go to the land of the gods. Tempest had no idea what would happen once they crossed over; she only knew that leaving him behind had not been an option.

Tempest chuckled to herself as she imagined the look on the members of his court's faces when they read the note they'd left behind. She'd found him in his room, and the two went through secret tunnels to prevent anyone from trying to stop them.

The relief in Aiden's eyes was apparent when they finally approached the temple. It was clear he thought they would never make it.

Up close, the temple was in bad shape. It looked like it had been through a war. There was sand and debris everywhere. It took Tempest a minute to find the entrance. She wasn't sure if it was because of the damage, or if it was just normally hidden.

The inside of the temple was dark and musty. Once Tempest's eyes adjusted, she could see that there were several passages leading off in different directions. She chose one randomly and started down it with Aiden following behind her. As they walked, she could feel the temperature drop. She was relieved to be out of the heat, but something about the cool air felt strange.

It had been so long since Tempest had last been here. Hundreds of years had faded her memory of where, precisely, the gate to the land of the gods was.

They had been walking for what felt like ages when Tempest began hearing a low buzzing from one side. They had to be getting close. She steered them towards the sound until an impossibly tall archway stood in front of them.

The archway was made of marble only a shade or two lighter than black, with gold carvings covering every inch of it. The designs were delicate and intricate, and Tempest's heart stirred as she recognized the craftsmanship of her people. She hadn't seen anything made by the denizens of the god realm for five hundred years. At first glance, the gilded etchings covering the archway looked similar to one another. Only upon a closer look could you make out the details, revealing images of creatures long forgotten, each more detailed and powerful than the next. The stone seems to flow like water around the images, giving the static edifice a sense of movement.

Tempest had always been in awe of such workmanship. As she studied archway more intently, she could feel a part of herself retreating into a corner of her mind. She shook her head and forced herself to focus on the task before her.

Noticing the fabric connecting her to Aiden had gone slack, she turned around to find him staring through the arch, his face devoid of emotion. His mind must have shut down upon reaching some mortal limit or reacting to the spells guarding the way to the land of the gods. Tempest gently took his hand and walked them through the gateway.

A cool breeze brushed past them, and Tempest felt her power respond, filling her with strength and energy.

They stood in a manicured forest. Tall marble buildings in the near distance peeked through the foliage. Beneath the canopy of trees, the ground was covered with emerald grass, which swayed in the wind. The smells of sweet grass and moist earth filled the air. The trees themselves were adorned in colorful fruits and flowers, adding a sweet, intoxicating scent. Branches hung over a path and brushed against one another, creating a cadence of clacking wood. The vibrant green leaves of the plants and trees rustled in a type of dance as they performed a melody that was effortless and yet difficult to understand. Regardless, it stirred the soul and brightened the mind.

Tempest closed her eyes and took a deep breath, swaying to the symphony of the forest. She loved the land of the gods. Even if you didn't know it was magical before arriving, you could feel it. If the other gods hadn't abused her powers, she never would have left.

She turned, curious and concerned about how Aiden would respond to this. His glazed-over expression morphed into one of peace, then pain, and last, confusion.

Aiden dropped the fabric from his hands and inspected them. "I feel... different."

"How so?"

"I feel strong and... something else I can't put my finger on."

"Can you describe it?"

"It keeps changing. Scared, then curious, and yet angry and loving under the surface."

Tempest cast a glance around to make sure they were still alone. "Does it feel like a cord? As if it's connecting you to something?"

A dimple appeared as his mouth quirked to the side while he thought. "Possibly?"

Tempest located the nearest moss-covered stone, then kicked it hard enough to bring tears to her eyes. Aiden flinched. She hopped on one foot and spun around to sit on the stone.

"I don't know how, but it appears this connection between us is no longer one-sided."

"*This* is what you've been feeling from me?"

"To an extent. Before, I was privy to your strongest emotions while you were oblivious to mine. Now you can feel mine. Personally, I've practiced to keep feelings tamped down. This is how I feel for every soul I'm near, experiencing their emotions in addition to my own."

Aiden's jaw dropped. "You can feel every soul near you? And all of their emotions?"

"It's sort of the worst." Tempest rose and tested her foot before putting her full weight on it. "We should go before someone discovers we are here."

"Where are we going?"

She began walking towards the marble buildings. "My place," she replied without looking back.

Tempest guided them around the outskirts of the buildings for a while. Aiden's eyes grew wider the further they went, as the buildings put his palace to shame, each structure grander than the last. They all stood at least five stories high, with a staircase leading from the courtyard to an upper terrace. Carvings and statues dotted the grounds, with large marble pillars supporting high archways leading inside.

Eventually, they left the forest and entered a broad path leading into a city of marble buildings. Tall walls surrounding individual structures rose on either side of them, with gates and doors providing entrance to them.

Tempest pushed against a large metal door with a beautiful woman holding scales etched onto it, and they entered a disheveled and barren courtyard. She closed the door behind them and walked towards a massive building in the center.

A small man in worn robes shuffled towards them, his face lighting up as he saw the goddess.

"It's good to have you home," the man said as he swept into a deep bow.

Tempest smiled. "It's good to be back, Verity. I'm a little surprised, though. My home does not look like the home of a god."

Verity rose and offered an apologetic smile. "You've been gone so long that all of your Broken have left me. Your residual power here has dwindled, and I've been left to care for your home as if I was a mere mortal."

Her brow rose as she looked around. "I shouldn't be surprised. I left with no warning and no plan of ever returning."

Verity nodded, glancing back and forth between her and Aiden. “You’ve brought a guest?”

“Ah, yes. This is Aiden. He is my guest and is under my protection. Please prepare a room for him beside mine. And Verity?”

“Yes, goddess?”

“Spread the word that I’ve returned. When you are done, I invite you to join us in the dining hall so we can catch up. I know how much you love gossip, and I’m sure you have plenty.”

Verity bowed again and left to do as his mistress ordered, practically bouncing on the balls of his feet.

Aiden watched as he disappeared into the mansion. “Your loyal servant?”

“Of a sort. I don’t actually have any servants. Sometimes those I’ve helped choose to stay on and serve me, to start a better life or just escape their old one. If they do stay, my residual power gives them a sort of protection. I guess I’ve been gone so long that was no longer the case for them.”

“You’re really not what I expected.”

Tempest strolled towards the entrance of her home. “You’ve known me long enough now that this is a surprise?”

Aiden took several quick steps to catch up and matched her pace. “No, but before that. I assumed all gods were power-hungry.”

“No, not all gods. We are much more like mortals than you would think. Sometimes we are corrupted by our immortality and power, though.”

"Why did you want Verity to spread the word you were here?"

A wicked grin spread across Tempest's face. "I'm sure a few of my Broken will find their way back, but truly, I want the gods who have been messing with you and the land of the mortals to tremble."

"You're that powerful?"

She chuckled. "They have no idea how powerful I really am, but from what they do know, they have every reason to fear me."

Chapter 22

Tempest led Aiden to the corner of a large dining hall. Tables and chairs filled the space in groups, with enough seating to comfortably feed over a hundred people.

With a happy sigh, she settled into an oversized plush red chair and gestured for Aiden to join her on one of the others around her. Verity soon walked in carrying a tray of food and drinks. He placed it on the low wooden table in the center of the grouping of chairs and took one for his own.

"You remembered my favorite. I'm touched." Tempest leaned forward and picked up a small round cookie flecked with yellow.

Verity picked one up and took a bite. "How could I forget? After years of harassing you for eating a cookie with a weed in it, you converted me yourself."

Aiden picked up a cookie and sniffed. "Do I want to know?"

"They're dandelion shortbread cookies. Really, they're delicious with all sorts of flowers and herbs added to them, but dandelion is my favorite. Especially with ginger tea and honey." Tempest took a bite, ignoring the crumbs as they fell to her chest. "Verity, these are as good as I remember."

"Thank you," Verity mumbled, averting his eyes as his face reddened.

Tempest poured herself a cup of tea and took a sip before continuing. "So, fill me in. What's happened recently?"

Verity set the rest of his cookie on the table and sat back in his chair. "It's not good. Kirata is missing."

Crumbs sprayed from Tempest's mouth as she coughed. "What?! The goddess of the heavens is missing? Who's running things right now?"

"Soleil and Aloysius, for the most part." Verity shrugged. "Who knew the gods of war and the sun would imprison Kirata? Wait, let me rephrase that—who knew *Soleil* would do this? Aloysius really isn't much of a surprise. He quite literally is the god of this sort of thing. No one knows where Kirata is or how they did it, though; just that suddenly, she was gone."

Aiden reached for a second cookie. "No wonder Soleil was able to keep the sun at its apex for days. There's no one to stop her."

Tempest thought for a moment. "That's not entirely true. Vesper is the god of the stars. He is her balance. Why isn't he doing anything about this?"

Verity shook his head. "No one knows. Your friend has always been a bit of a recluse. I haven't seen or heard anything from him or the god of the dead."

Tempest's eyes darted to Aiden and then back to the cup of tea in her hand. "I've heard from the god of the dead recently. He can't help."

"Oh?" Verity leaned forward, his elbows on his knees.

She smirked and raised a hand to halt him. "I'm not going there." Turning to Aiden, she said, "I suggest after we finish here, we visit Vesper and see what's going on."

He nodded in agreement, his mouth full of cookie.

Tempest knocked a fourth time on the entrance to Vesper's home and received no response. After a quick look to make sure the coast was clear, she motioned for Aiden to come over. "Give me a boost," she whispered.

"You can't be serious, Tempest," Aiden whispered back.

"Since when did you start questioning a god?"

"When that god started making bad choices. We are not breaking into another god's home. Especially the god of time!"

"He's a big softie," Tempest scoffed, "and he won't mind if we're the ones breaking in."

"What do you mean 'we'? He doesn't know me."

She shaded her eyes and looked up at the top of the wall. "Nothing, just a common way of speaking." Tempest cleared her throat. "Hurry up and help me."

Locking his fingers together and opening his hands, Aiden supported Tempest as she stepped into his hands and pulled herself to the top of the wall. Straddling it, she dropped her hand and waved it for Aiden to grasp.

"You can't be serious."

Footsteps echoed off the walls from around the corner.

"You're more likely to be caught out here without me than you are in here with me."

Aiden took her hand, and with a grunt, she pulled him over the wall. His foot slipped on the marble, and both toppled off the wall inside the courtyard. Aiden was sprawled on top of Tempest, and their eyes locked. Shock and need zipped through her connection from him, and she froze. They lay there as the footsteps walked past Vesper's door and disappeared.

Tempest gently moved her hands between them and pushed him off, breaking the tension.

Aiden looked down at her. "That was close," he said, his voice rough.

Tempest nodded, her heart pounding in her chest. She could feel the attraction between them, the electric pull that made her want to close the space between them and kiss him. But she didn't—she couldn't. Aiden was off-limits, no matter how much her body wanted him. Although he was technically a god, he was still undergoing a mortal trial.

Aiden stood up and offered her a hand. Tempest cleared her throat and took it. Standing, she turned around and pointed towards the main entrance. She started walking, her heart still racing and her mind unable to process words just yet.

Inside, everything looked the same as the last time she was there—the statues, paintings, carvings, and even the tapestries that hung on the walls. Vesper's home was as she remembered it, nothing out of place.

"Vesper?" she called, walking up the steps.

Aiden stopped in the entryway, his hands on his hips as his eyes took in the room.

Tempest walked on. A shiver ran down the back of her neck as her blood traveled from her limbs to her heart.

"There's no one here," Aiden said.

"Maybe he headed towards the cliffs to..."

Tempest's voice trailed off as the door burst open. She turned and tensed as two men walked in, wearing the red and black uniform and swords of Vesper's guards. One carried a letter sealed with Vesper's stamp while the other held a necklace with a small key.

Both bowed as they approached Tempest. "Goddess, we have been expecting you."

Puzzled, Tempest waited for them to rise and continue.

Hand outstretched, the man with the letter continued, "Our master is out and will be for some time, but he left these in our care for when you returned."

She took the items and watched as the two men bowed again and retreated, leaving Tempest and Aiden alone again.

"What is it?"

Tempest shrugged as she looked at the key. Something about it was familiar, but she couldn't determine why, exactly. She looped the necklace over her head and cracked the wax seal on the letter.

Tempest,

I am sure you are confused, and I'm afraid I can't explain everything just yet. I'm glad you are safe and have reconnected with Aiden. By now, you've discovered who he really is, as well as what has happened in the land of the gods.

When Aiden first came to me wanting a mortal trial, I refused. The land of the dead cannot be left unguarded. If another god gained control over it, it would tip the scales of power. Any god who is willing to do that is not one I can let be in power.

Strange things are happening, though, and Aiden was convinced the land of the dead was being targeted. Because he had not done a mortal trial for much longer than the other gods, he was afraid he would be too weak to stop them. I agreed to send him secretly and stand guard for him over his domain. I've left his true name and a loophole in his trial in case things went awry so you two would be reconnected. I only hope he is not an infant when the two of you meet.

Soon after he left, I was called to a mortal trial of my own. When I return, I will explain myself to you both and face the consequences, but know it was not a decision I took lightly.

Before you left the land of the gods, you entrusted me with something and made me swear to protect it with my life until you returned. You had me clear all memory of it from your mind. I have brought it with me to my mortal trial so it will stay safe, but left the key to open it with my men to protect it from any unexpected mishaps.

You are the goddess of the broken, and our home is broken. If you are reading this, it means things have gone wrong in ways I saw but hoped would never happen. Find it in your heart to forgive those who deserve it and reclaim your throne.

I need you. Aiden needs you. Both the lands of the gods and mortals need you.

Your Friend,

Vesper

Aiden's voice cut through Tempest's thoughts. "What does it say?"

She closed the letter and tucked it in her pocket. "He's gone and can't be of any help to us."

"What do we do?"

"We find Kirata."

Laughter and music filled Tempest's ears as she approached Amais's home. The god of love threw the best parties. His temple was always filled with music and laughter. It was a contrast to the somber atmosphere of some of the other temples, and Tempest couldn't help but feel a twinge of jealousy. She quickly pushed the feeling aside; she had no time for such things.

"Why are we here?" Aiden asked, looking around at the revelers.

"I made a promise to someone," Tempest replied, her eyes scanning the crowd. "Keep your head down. Mortals are not welcome in this realm. I want to get in and get out without causing a fuss."

The two entered the gate and faced the assembly of gods and god-touched beings. It was an ocean of color and movement as gowns swirled and servers carried trays of food and drink. Music played in the background, masking the noise of the crowd with a fast beat, the synergy of the rhythm reminiscent of excitement and desire.

Tempest scanned the crowd for the chief gods. She found Ruyah, goddess of sleep and dreams, leaning against a column with a glass of wine in hand as she gazed indifferently at the group surrounding a table near her. Her white hair, brows, and lashes were as pale as her personality.

Tynan, god of chaos and luck, sat at a table with Bramble, goddess of fertility and harvest, and Septimus, god of luck, arguing with golden chalices in hand. If gods had parents, one would assume those three were siblings. Their ink black hair, pale skin, and rosy lips were eerily similar. Even from a distance, Tempest could see not much had changed among them in the years she'd been gone. She could almost hear their argument—Tynan complaining that he was also a god of luck and should receive due reverence, and the other two accusing him of being only bad luck and not requiring it; after all, he was the god of chaos. In truth, Tynan used his luck much more frequently than Septimus. He truly was more powerful; he was just unable to control what kind of luck he gave. It frustrated him to no end.

Tempest turned her attention back to the crowd, but she didn't see Amias anywhere. She nodded toward a building and led Aiden through the crowd towards it.

It was a radiant shrine, lavishly decorated with swirls of lily and daffodil and gilded with ivy. The floors were as red as a bleeding heart, and statues lined the walls, lit by flickering torches. One in particular caught Tempest's eye. In it, Amias was depicted in garb the colors of cornflower and blood, an image of herself clinging to his leg.

Tempest's stomach turned. This was an addition after she had left, and a brilliant reminder of why she had abandoned the land of the gods to begin with. While Amias had stayed on good terms with her most of the time, they had never been lovers, nor had she ever been subservient to him, as this projected.

Someone approached Tempest, and to her surprise, Zarya, goddess of the sea, stood there, arms crossed over her curvy body. The blue of her eyes glowed slightly as it twisted, revealing the storm within.

"Look who decided to quit playing mortal."

Tempest turned to face the goddess, putting herself between Zarya and Aiden as she did so.

"No playing. I just needed a change of pace."

Zarya's eyes darted between Tempest and Aiden with a knowing look. "It appears you found one. For having been gone so long, you've put on quite the show. How did you like Aloysius's present?"

"What present?"

"The dragon. How did you not know it was him? He has a whole valley full of them that he's raised since they were eggs."

That was news to Tempest. It did explain why only she had run into the dragon.

"It certainly made an impression."

Tempest studied Zarya. What did she want? She was always a fairly neutral god, never that close to anyone. Instead, she chose her lovers from the beings who lived in her domain outside the main grouping of the gods' homes. No one knew how many children the woman really had, only that she claimed just the most powerful ones.

"I'm surprised to see you here. I thought you never came to these parties," Tempest said.

"I'm here for you, actually."

Aiden cleared his throat, and Zarya's eyes darted to him before turning back to Tempest. A knot formed in Tempest's stomach.

"I hear you're looking for your friend," Zarya continued.

"What makes you think that?" How did she know?

"You're not the only one with connections, my dear." The goddess's tone changed. "They had to break her, you know. To take her. They wore her down, and you weren't here to fix her, so she became weak."

She had to be talking about Kirata.

"At first, it was only small things. She let them roll off her back. You know how confident she's always been; both a gift and a curse, really. When they started to crack her shell though, she had no one to turn to. Everyone was too afraid of what would happen to them. You have to fix this as only you can."

"I don't know how yet."

"There's always a way. The earth and sea speak to me without words. I know how to read them. They showed me how to find her. You just need to listen."

"That makes no sense."

"My friend, is that really any of my concern?" Zarya replied with a soft laugh. "Fix yourself and stop running."

Tempest could tell the matter was closed. She wasn't going to get a clearer answer from her.

Zarya started to walk away. Tempest grabbed her wrist. "Thank you."

Zarya smiled as Tempest released her. It was a genuine one, and gave Tempest hope.

A voice rang out. "Tempest!"

It was Amias. Tempest reluctantly made her way to where he stood near a group of cushions, stopping a few feet in front of him. She eyed the group of sprites and nymphs sprawled across the cushions, who were giggling as if drunk.

"Hello, Amias," she replied.

Shaggy brown hair partially covering his eyes, the God of Love lazily waved at her. "You are looking well. Long time, no see. What brings you here?"

"Do you really need to ask?"

The dimples of his coy smile on his perfect olive face told her that he knew, but wanted her to say it. He wanted a challenge.

"Did you use the same thing on them as you did on your representative?" Tempest asked, gesturing to Amias's entourage.

"I didn't need to. I simply exude love."

"You do? That's new. Since when did you start forcing love instead of encouraging true bonds to form?"

Amias shifted his gaze to Aiden. "When I quit being able to see them."

"What?! How did that happen?"

He shrugged. "No idea. Only that it happened not too long ago; around the same time your friends went into seclusion."

Tempest thought about Vesper. He rarely did mortal trials, and if things weren't set up properly before he left, it could have accidentally caused this. He not only set up mortal trials for the gods, but also the ones for the mortals themselves.

"Ah." She didn't really know how to respond without giving too much away.

"You really didn't bring who I think you brought to one of my parties, did you? I thought you knew the rules. No lessers allowed. The food and drink alone could have dire consequences."

"I know. We aren't staying. I needed to see you personally, though."

His hand dropped to the head of a woman beside him, and his fingers twirled in her hair. "Oh? I'm intrigued."

"I'm asking you to release your representative from your deal. Let her follow her own fate for her love match."

His hand froze. "You think you have that much sway over me? You've been gone so long you must have forgotten where you stand among the gods."

She laced her response with her power. "And you seem to have forgotten that I chose to be there."

He cleared his throat and shifted. "Apparently. If you can find a way to fix this," he gestured to himself, "so I can use my power, and not just leak it everywhere like a dog in heat, I will release her. I will even help her."

"Thank you."

With a small nod, she turned on her heel, shoulders back, head held high, and began to walk away. "Also," she added as she waved over her shoulder, "get rid of that ridiculous statue before I destroy it myself."

"Tempest!"

She and Aiden both turned to see a girl of no more than sixteen running towards them, her blonde hair flying behind her in a wild mass.

"Do you know her?" Aiden asked.

"She's one of my Broken. Word that I've returned has spread faster than I anticipated," Tempest answered.

The girl finally caught up to them and bent over, trying to catch her breath.

"What's wrong?" Tempest asked.

"It's Toph," she said between breaths. "There's an army...approaching it. Soleil and Aloysius...are trying to breach the gates...and claim the throne...of the god of the dead."

Fear clutched Tempest's chest, and for a moment, she couldn't breathe. If they claimed Toph, they would be unstoppable. They would become the most powerful gods, no matter which one of them came out on top and took the power that came with the throne.

She looked at Aiden. "I need you to go back to my temple and stay there until this is over."

"What? No! I can fight." Aiden grabbed Tempest's arm.

"You are mortal!" Tempest spat back. "You would only hinder me."

"No; you cannot fight alone. I may be mortal, but I am not afraid to fight a god."

She ripped her arm from his grip. "That just shows how much of a fool you truly are. You couldn't last against one god, let alone two, with an entire army of demigods and magical beings at their backs."

"And you can?"

She glared at him, feeling the anger rolling from him through their connection. Straightening her back and tossing her head, she replied, "I don't have to win; I just have to stop them."

"That's suicide!"

"That's what life is like in the land of the gods!"

They stared each other down until a squeak broke the silence. Both heads whipped towards the Broken, who cowered beneath their intense gazes.

"Go with her and stay with her at my temple," Tempest commanded, pointing to the girl. "That is my decision, and it's final."

She turned her back to them, called her power, and spirited towards Toph, her body disappearing in a cloud of blue smoke. Searing pain ripped through her gut as her rapid travel suddenly stopped and her body slammed onto the hard ground. She groaned as she rolled over and realized her mistake. The pain so intense she could barely move, she spirited back to where she had left Aiden, appearing next to the writhing mortal emperor.

"I'm so sorry; I don't know what happened!" the blonde girl apologized, sobbing. "He just cried out and dropped to the ground."

Tempest sat up and reached out to touch Aiden. He flinched away from her.

"It's okay. I'm not going to hurt you."

Barely looking away from Aiden's curled-up body, Tempest told the girl, "Go back to my temple and tell them what is happening. Tell them I am heading to Toph to stop it, and anyone who can help needs to answer my call."

The girl bowed, her hair nearly touching the ground, then straightened and ran as fast as she could in the direction of Tempest's temple.

"Aiden, I'm sorry. I wasn't thinking. I was worried about Toph and forgot about the connection between us. Are you all right?"

Aiden slowly rose, first to his knees and finally onto his feet, his body still quivering. Tempest looked up at the man standing in front of her. How she hadn't known who he was immediately, she could only guess. The sun shining behind him recreated the crown she'd seen when they first met.

He offered his hand and helped pull her up. "Never do that again."

"I promise."

Aiden began to pull his hand away, but Tempest gripped it tighter. "Not yet. I need to be in physical contact with you to have you travel with me."

"Like you just did?"

She nodded. "It's something gods can only do in the land of the gods—well, except Kirata, she can do it anywhere—but it comes in handy. You ready?"

He gave her a single nod, despite being pale and looking like he was about to be sick.

She hoped the smile she gave him was more reassuring than how she felt inside. She pictured Toph's gates in her mind, and a moment later, only a few wisps of blue smoke were left where the two had been standing.

When Tempest and Aiden appeared at the edge of the valley, they had only a moment to glimpse the valley of Toph.

It was a never-ending gray valley with a black stone wall extending as far as the eye could see in both directions, each stone the size of a house. The enormous gates stood in the center of the valley, made of obsidian with a jagged crack down the middle, carved deeply with symbols that looked red as blood. The moans of the souls of the dead were the only sounds coming from beyond the wall.

An army of magical beings fought outside the gate. The attackers were short and ugly, with long, sharp teeth and colorful hats on their heads. Their armor was made of splintered bones, gray as ashes, adorned with ornaments made of frozen tears and ribbons of skin. This was the army of Aloysius.

Demigod warriors fought alongside them, bedecked in gleaming armor that shone as brightly as a star. The army of Soleil shone on the battlefield. Those brave and tactically superior demigod warriors could tear moving water into knots of steam and freeze flying sand into glass armor.

The horde spanned the valley, and their numbers were so great that one could not see the end of this fighting force.

Toph's army seemed beautiful in comparison to the others, shining in their black and silver armor. Although they moved faster than their attackers, they were severely outnumbered. Tempest saw no way for them to win this battle alone.

She scanned the battlefield, looking for the gods behind the bloodbath. A bright flash of light revealed Soleil, soldiers laid out several rows deep in a circle around her after the blast.

Raising her finger to point out the goddess to Aiden, she nudged his elbow and moved towards the battle.

"Stay close," she commanded.

Aiden nodded and drew a blade from his hip. As unprepared as he had been for traveling to the land of the gods, Tempest was grateful that he had insisted on bringing his own blade.

The familiar warmth of Soulshadow's chains graced Tempest's hands as she called it.

A golden warrior noticed them as they approached the edge of the battle and charged at them with a cry, gaining the attention of several others.

Tempest sent Soulshadow's chain at the first attacker's leg. As it wrapped around the man's calf and hooked onto itself, she pulled the man off his feet and dragged him towards her. She swung the excess chain in her opposite hand behind her and, with a heavy arch, impaled the ball and spikes into his chest. With a flick of her wrist, she called her weapon back to and targeted her next victim.

She turned to check where Aiden had moved to and found him using his blade to decapitate one of their foes. He moved on to his next victim without losing momentum. If she weren't in the throes of a battle, she would have found it mesmerizing and beautiful, in a very twisted way.

The two slowly worked their way through the battlefield towards Soleil. Occasional flashes of her attacks guided their way.

A large half-man, half-beast stopped both of them in their tracks. Those around them immediately backed away as if they were afraid of him as well, even those who were his allies.

His upper body was that of a heavily-muscled man, his face brutal and savage. His lower body, however, was of a scaled monster with thighs thick like tree trunks, his calves larger than Tempest's waist. A tail coiled behind him, ready to strike with its metal tip. His eyes narrowed as he rushed them with a hiss.

Aiden rolled to the left and immediately got back onto his feet, avoiding the attack. Tempest swung Soulshadow towards the man's left arm as she jumped out of the way. The beast's tail swatted her chain away and struck Tempest's side, slamming her to the ground.

Aiden ran forward and sliced at the man's calf, but his sword bounced off scales. He tried again, aiming towards the man's torso, but his blade was flicked from his hand by that infernal tail. Aiden stumbled back a few steps, caught off-balance. Before he could regain his footing, the metal tip at the end of the tail pierced his chest.

Tempest screamed as she ran towards him, each step seeming to drag on for an eternity. The light disappeared from Aiden's eyes as he watched her trying to reach him. Before his blood could even reach the ground, his body turned to dust and drifted away on a gust of wind.

Chapter 23

The man-beast roared in triumph before turning his attention to Tempest.

She was livid. Every ounce of pain Aiden had felt in his death, she had felt as well, until their connection snapped and vanished.

Tempest saw the world in shades of black and white, splashes of red blood the only color. Her mind was becoming unhinged, and she embraced it.

She was the goddess of the broken. Her power boiled inside her, begging to be set free and seek vengeance. It demanded retribution for this moment.

Hand poised as a claw before her, Tempest stood still as the beast charged her. She called his soul to her hand.

He stopped abruptly.

Gathering the soul in her palm, she looked over at the beast, who was hardly keeping upright. The soul's dusty essence slowly snaked its way between the beast's ribs as she watched. Tempest's mouth stretched into a broad smile, and for a moment, she could see the strain in the soul as it fought against the force pulling it away from its host.

She closed her hand into a tight fist and snuffed out the life that had been in it a moment before. The ground shook as the man-beast collapsed, never to rise again.

Tempest's smile faded as she turned her attention back to the fighting. She was alone in the middle of a battle, and she had a goddess to defeat.

She once again scanned the battlefield. Soleil and her army were pushing the line of Toph's army further and further towards the gate.

A rustle of cloth and the clink of armor rang out behind her. She turned, but found no one there. A tingling sensation on the back of her neck had her spinning around again.

Soleil appeared in front of her, sword at the ready. Tempest's brow furrowed as she felt her eyes widen, her mouth open and shut, but no words left her lips. She had never seen anything like Soleil's sword. It was long and curved, and the hilt was made of gold encrusted with rubies and diamonds, the blade etched with symbols and scenes of battles that Tempest was unfamiliar with.

Where did Soleil get such a magnificent sword? How could she wield such a weapon? Why hadn't she used it before?

Soleil charged while she was distracted. Tempest dodged and began circling the golden goddess.

"You are all alone. The runaway goddess has no one. Do you really think you have a chance?" Soleil taunted.

"Who said I'm alone? Don't you see the army surrounding me?"

Soleil tsked. "You and I both know the denizens of Toph aren't your army."

Tempest wanted to wipe the smug look off of Soleil's perfect face. The goddess of the sun's worshipers swore she was so beautiful that if you looked her directly in the eyes, you would go blind.

Tempest knew that under the perfect facade was an ordinary woman. She didn't like that the sun goddess she knew before had become twisted and dark. Gone was the woman who filled her role because she cared for her people. Soleil's soul was almost unrecognizable.

"Don't you dare judge me," Soleil hissed as she swung her sword at Tempest's torso. "I know that look."

Tempest jumped back and knocked the sword away with Soulshadow. She gave Soleil a wide smile. "I wasn't judging you; I was admiring your beauty."

Soleil's face contorted with a rage. "Liar!"

Tempest covered her mouth with her hand, spluttering as she choked back a fit of giggles. She had to put all of her self-control into not to sniggering at Soleil's little tantrum and the look on her face. She knew she was in no position to be laughing, and yet, she couldn't help it.

Soleil's eyes flashed, and she knocked Tempest to the ground with a blast of light from her free hand.

Tempest coughed as she pushed herself off of the ground. While she looked whole, she wasn't fully repaired yet. Her body was still recovering from the injuries she had received before.

The sun goddess's face relaxed, but her eyes still shone with anger. "What's so funny?"

"You. I was laughing at your face," Tempest answered with a smile.

Soleil scowled. "Why?"

"It's easier than fighting you. You have a beautiful face, but your heart is ugly. Aloysius has twisted you. Why do you follow him?" Tempest asked. She was curious if Soleil was aware of the war god's plans.

The sun goddess's eyes narrowed. "How dare you question my motives? He is the god of war. He was the only one who didn't see me as monotonous. How could I not follow him? Besides, he is out of your league. He is so much more powerful than you can imagine."

"Do you believe he will win the war?" Tempest asked.

A flash of gold caught Tempest's eye as the two circled each other. A golden necklace in the shape of an egg hung from a delicate chain around Soleil's neck. Why did it seem familiar?

"Of course, he will," Soleil answered with a haughty smile. "He is the strongest god."

"The strongest god is not always the winner. How much can the strongest god do if you are his only follower? There's a reason Kirata is the goddess of the heavens," Tempest replied.

"You're wrong. He will win because he is the strongest. The only one who can defeat him is another god of equal power, and there is none."

Tempest laughed. "I can promise you, he is not the most powerful god."

"You think you are?"

Tempest chose not to answer, her focus on the necklace. Why couldn't she remember it when clearly there was something to be remembered? Vesper's letter came to mind. He had wiped her memory; maybe the necklace was part of that.

Soulshadow swung at Soleil's feet, kicking up dust as the spikes dragged on the ground. The chain wrapped around the sun goddess's feet, and with a quick pull, she lay on the ground.

Tempest felt a rush of satisfaction run through her veins as her patience was rewarded. She had so much anger for Soleil, and she wasn't going to hold back.

Soleil met Tempest's eyes, surprising her with a small smirk. "Good. This is what I wanted. I wanted to see you fall."

Tempest scowled in confusion. "What did you say?"

Soleil closed her eyes. "Rest, little goddess. Rest and dream about what could have been."

The ground beneath Tempest began to shake, and she was lifted into the air. Soleil's eyes opened, and the immense power behind them made Tempest's skin crawl. The ground started to move. Sparks of white light surrounded Tempest, and she could feel something pulling her power from her. It was like a curtain had been closed.

A deafening roar shook the area, and Tempest looked to the source. The gates of Toph groaned open. Spirits of the dead poured over the walls, ripping the souls of those they encountered from their bodies and pulling them back into Toph.

Tempest struggled to be released from Soleil's power while the sun goddess was distracted, but she failed.

Through the gates, a single man emerged. Black wisps of power flicked from him, attacking the soldiers nearest the gate. Each one dropped immediately once touched.

A wicked grin spread across Tempest's face as she realized who it was.

"Are you sure Aloysius is the strongest god? The god of the dead judges the souls of the departed while I judge the souls of the living. None can escape us."

Soleil glared at Tempest. "Oh, you think so?"

She shook her feet free of Soulshadow's chains, and the ball and chain disappeared. Tempest tried to call it back, but couldn't access it. Panic hit her, and she looked earnestly back at the god of the dead.

Aiden was rushing towards her, his power wiping out entire sections of Soleil's and Aloysius's armies along his path. For a moment, Tempest felt hope. Aiden had ended his mortal trial and regained his full godly powers.

Bright light from Soleil's neck distracted Tempest as she felt her body being pulled towards the necklace. The egg opened, and no matter how hard Tempest fought against it, she couldn't escape.

Aiden roared as he got close enough to grab Tempest, but the necklace pulled her in just as his hand reached hers. Soleil's cackle and Aiden's terrified face were the last things she heard and saw before the egg closed. She was trapped.

The first thing Tempest became aware of was the sound of her own breathing. She could feel her chest heaving as she breathed large gulps of air as if she'd been holding her breath for a very long time.

Tempest opened her eyes and tried to sit up, but was unable to move. She was trapped in some sort of cocoon made from her own power. She sent out a tendril of power to try and break free, but it only rebounded back off the walls of her prison, weakening her further.

A vision of Aiden appeared before her, his eyes full of pain and anger. He reached out to touch her, but his hand passed through hers as if she wasn't there.

"Aiden," she whispered, not knowing if he could hear her or not.

The vision disappeared and was replaced by one of herself, wearing a white gown dripping in blood. It was the one she had started the Dei Electi in.

The blood from her dress pooled in the bottom of the cocoon until the weight ripped through. Tempest fell out of the base into a swirl of cloud so thick she couldn't find her own feet. The only sign she was still falling was the fabric of her dress whipping her face.

Suddenly, her fall was stopped, although she was still surrounded by darkness. She silently called out for Aiden, but couldn't find a way out of the darkness. She didn't know where she was. Tempest closed and opened her eyes again, hoping to see some light, but she was still trapped in darkness.

"Hello?"

A bright light pierced through the darkness, but it wasn't white. It was orange.

Tempest blinked as the light grew brighter, blinding her. The light and heat got stronger and stronger, threatening to burst through and engulf her essence entirely. Her body began to burn, and she could feel her skin cracking.

She heard a loud crack, and a blazing wave hit her all at once.

A woman rushed towards her, ax in hand, and swung at Tempest's head. Tempest tried to call Soulshadow, but it didn't respond. She dropped to her knees and rolled out of the ax's path.

The woman disappeared, taking the light with her.

Ears alert for any sound of movement, Tempest began crawling through the dark slowly, one hand in front of the other, so she didn't run into anything. Tempest had no way to track time and began counting her movements.

Left, two hundred thirty-two.

Right, two hundred thirty-three

Left, two hundred thirty-four.

Right... She stopped. Picked her hand back up and put it back down harder. It splashed in water. She moved her left hand forward, and it splashed, as well. The water began to glow as if sensing it was her, and a vision appeared within it.

Tempest felt herself being pulled into the water and saw herself sitting in a tree with Aiden. They were staring at the stars, and she leaned against him, feeling his warmth. She felt safe, valued.

"I love you, Tempest," Aiden whispered, his breath tickling her ear.

Tempest froze, her heart pounding in her chest. She was scared to say anything, scared that if she spoke, the spell would be broken, and this moment would be gone.

Aiden must have sensed her hesitation, because he spoke again. "I know you're scared, but I want you to know that I love you. I'll always love you."

Tempest felt tears well up in her eyes, and she turned to face him. "I love you, too," she said before throwing her arms around him and burying her face in his chest.

"I wish we could stay like this forever," she said softly.

"Me, too," Aiden replied, gently stroking her hair. "But sadly, we can't."

Suddenly, the image changed, and she saw herself lying on the ground, blood pooling around her. Aiden was leaning over her, tears in his eyes.

"No," Tempest whispered, shaking her head. "No, no, no."

These were memories. Her memories. She realized then why the necklace Soleil wore was so familiar. It had been Tempest's. Only, Tempest didn't own it anymore. She had locked away the memories she needed to forget to go to the land of the mortals and given it to Vesper. All of the most painful memories, and the ones that made her question her decision, were in this necklace.

She looked back at Aiden, holding her limp body. This had been her last straw. A petty fight between several of the gods had resulted in this. She was always called in to mediate the conflicts and punish the losing god or gods, but they had cheated and turned on her when she ruled against them.

Tempest could feel the anger she'd felt at the betrayal wash over her as she reclaimed the memory. Aiden had found her like this after the other gods were done with her.

She tried to escape the vision, but it was like being trapped in quicksand. The more she fought, the deeper she sank.

The image changed again, and she saw Aiden walking away from her, his back straight and his steps purposeful.

He didn't look back once.

"Aiden!" Tempest called, but he didn't hear her.

Her heart broke as she relived the memory. She'd just told Aiden her plan to leave; asked him to come with her, but he couldn't. She knew he couldn't. Toph needed him, and it had been selfish to ask. Tempest was too broken then to understand what she was really asking him to do.

She tried to follow, but her feet were stuck in place.

The image faded as a ripple bounced across the surface of the water.

An ax swung in front of her. Tempest looked up to find the woman from before towering over her. The woman's laugh was manic and insane, her raven-black hair ratted as if her fingers had ravaged it in a moment of distress. She breathed heavily, as if demanding Tempest fight her.

"Kirata?" Tempest whispered.

The woman standing before her was the image of Kirata, but she seemed so different.

"Come on," the goddess of the heavens said, almost as if she could read Tempest's mind.

"What's happening?" Tempest asked.

Kirata looked sorrowful. "It's happening."

Tempest scrambled to her feet, and the woman disappeared.

Darkness descended around her.

Tempest could hear her own screams from behind her, but couldn't see where they were coming from. As she walked forward, she found herself surrounded by both her own and Aiden's memories. When she first met Aiden, when Aiden first met her, when they first kissed, every day that Tempest had with Aiden played in front of her.

"Stop," Tempest shouted, but the memories didn't heed her.

"Stop!" she shouted again, but the images continued.

A hand closed around Tempest's wrist, jerking her forward.

"You can't stop this. This is a prison of your own making, one that Soleil and Aloysius have trapped me in," Kirata said.

"I'm sorry. I didn't mean to make this into a prison for other gods. I just needed to escape."

Kirata gripped Tempest's wrist tighter. "None of us can truly escape our past or our fate. I've been trapped here and seen what they have done to you; what you allowed them to do to you."

"What?! I had no choice!"

"You always have a choice," Kirata spat. "You are the goddess of the broken! You deliver vengeance for the living. When will you deliver vengeance for yourself? Are you not one of the living?"

Tempest chose not to answer. She was seething inside. How dare Kirata tell her she was in the wrong for needing to escape? To get away from the abuse she received from those more powerful than her?

Suddenly, she stopped.

Hadn't she just told Soleil that she wasn't a weak god? That she should be feared?

"We should keep going. We're almost there," Kirata said from the dark as she tugged Tempest's arm.

Tempest followed. "Where are we going?"

"The exit."

"If you knew where the exit was, why didn't you escape yourself?"

"You really think I didn't try?" Kirata scoffed. "I don't have the key."

"What key?"

Kirata stopped, and Tempest ran into her back.

"What do you mean, what key? Did you not bring it with you? Aren't you here to save me?"

"I was looking for you and planned to save you, but Soleil trapped me in here first."

Kirata growled. "Fine. Let's get to the exit, and we'll figure out what to do there."

The two continued walking, and soon something appeared, glowing in the distance. As they drew closer, Tempest could make out a wooden jewelry box on a table made of gold.

Kirata led Tempest to it and dropped her hand.

"This is it?" Tempest asked, confused.

"Were you expecting more?"

"Maybe a door or archway... something we could fit within."

Kirata raised her brow and gave Tempest a look that made her feel as if she was a child. "You're the one who made this, and you question the decision?"

Tempest blushed and scratched her head. "Good point."

Upon closer inspection, the box was simple, made of highly polished dark wood and a small golden latch with a lock on it keep it closed.

A sharp sting over her heart made Tempest flinch. She reached up to grab her chest, surprised when something hard hit her fingertips. Tempest reached inside her dress and pulled out the small key Vesper had left her.

She looked from the key to the box on the table and smiled. "Let's get out of here. I've got work to do."

Kirata laughed. "There's the goddess of the broken I've been waiting for. Let's do this."

Chapter 24

Tempest inserted the key into the lock and turned. There was a click, and the latch sprang open. She lifted the lid of the box, revealing a swirling mass of light inside.

"That's it?" Kirata asked skeptically.

"You expected something else?" Tempest replied.

She took Kirata's hand. "Hold on tight. This might be a bumpy ride."

Kirata nodded, and Tempest reached into the box. The light swirled around them, enveloping them in its brightness. Tempest could feel Kirata's hand gripping hers tightly as they were pulled forward. Suddenly, the light vanished, and they were standing in a dark forest.

"Where are we?" Kirata asked, looking around.

"I'm not sure," Tempest replied.

She stepped forward, and her foot sank into the soft earth beneath her. As she pulled it back out, she noticed her foot was covered in blood.

"Tempest, look," Kirata said, pointing.

Tempest's gaze followed Kirata's finger, and she saw bodies strewn about the ground. Some looked as if they had been there for years, while others looked fresh.

"What is this place?" Kirata whispered.

"I think we just found the answer to your question," Tempest replied. "This is the underworld, Toph."

"How did we end up here?"

Tempest looked more closely at the bodies around them. Most were from the army of Soleil and Aloysius. How had they gotten inside the gates?

A glint of gold caught her eye. Tempest squatted down and picked up a dainty chain from the ground. A golden egg followed out from under the arm of a body.

"Is that..."

Tempest nodded. "It's our prison."

She pocketed the necklace and looked around to get her bearings. The walls of Toph stood in the distance behind them, and a mountain towered over them.

"This way," Tempest said confidently as she stepped forward.

Kirata hesitated. "You're sure?"

Tempest angled her head towards the mountain. "I'm guessing you've never been to Toph before. I used to spend a lot of time here. The god of the dead's home is in the mountain."

Tempest led Kirata towards a river nearby. A group of Aiden's soldiers stood on the bank, throwing corpses into the river to allow them to travel to the underworld and find their rest.

She kept a close eye on Kirata. The goddess of the heavens she remembered was so different, much more confident and intimidating. Tempest would have wondered what happened to cause the change, but now that she could remember everything she had trapped within the egg, she knew exactly what had broken the goddess of the heavens.

It had broken Tempest herself, and she was *made* to take on others' emotions and problems. Kirata wasn't, and had been trapped there.

"Goddess," one of Aiden's men called out as he noticed her. He ran and knelt before her. "We thought you were dead."

"As you can see, I'm not, although Soleil certainly tried her best," Tempest replied.

The man got to his feet and gestured for her to follow him. "Come; my Lord Aiden will want to see you."

An empty ebony boat floated down the river until it came to a stop at the edge in front of them. The man gestured for the two women to climb in and joined them in the boat. Tempest sat down as the boat floated towards the mountain.

The silence was deafening. Tempest had never traveled through Toph without Aiden and found it unsettling.

The boat stopped before a large cave opening, and Tempest helped Kirata climb out of the boat. After a quick wave goodbye, the two entered the mountain.

"Stay close to me, Kirata. There are beings in this mountain that only answer to Aiden. We do not want to run into them."

Kirata nodded her understanding and followed closely behind.

The cave grew brighter as they ventured deeper into the mountain. A small group of Aiden's men stood in the center of a vast cavern. One of them noticed Tempest and made to rush towards her. He stopped when she held her hand up. Tempest held her finger to her lips to indicate they should be quiet.

The man nodded and turned back to the group, whispering something to them. Tempest nodded to the man, and he waved them forward. Tempest led Kirata around the group and into the small entrance a short distance from them. Aiden was sitting at a table in the next room, his head in his hands.

"Aiden," Tempest said softly as she walked towards him.

He looked up, then stood and hugged her.

"Tempest!"

Aiden held her tightly, his relief evident in his embrace. He brushed her hair back from her face and looked down at her.

"I thought I'd lost you," he whispered.

Tempest shook her head. "I'm here; I'm fine."

Aiden cupped her face in his hands and kissed her gently. Tempest melted into him, returning the kiss with as much passion as he gave.

Finally, they pulled apart, both of them breathing heavily.

"I'm so glad you're okay," Aiden said, his voice rough with emotion.

"I am, too," Tempest replied.

They stood there for a moment, just looking at each other. Finally, Aiden broke the silence.

"I have something for you," he said, stepping away from Tempest and walking towards a tunnel leading away from the room.

Tempest called one of the guards over before following Aiden and gestured at Kirata. "Take care of her. If anything happens to her, your life will be forfeit."

The guard's face turned white, but he nodded quickly.

Tempest hurried to catch up to Aiden and locked her fingers with his. His surprised look quickly melted.

"You remember?" he asked.

"Everything. I'm so incredibly sorry for what I've put you through."

"We can talk about that later. For now, we have other important things that need to be taken care of."

She followed him through the winding tunnel deeper into the mountain. Goosebumps rose on her arm as it grew colder the farther they went.

Aiden led Tempest into a room off the side of the tunnel, and Tempest gasped. Soleil hung from the wall, chains wrapped around her legs and wrists.

"Don't worry. She can't escape. The chains block a god's magic. She is as weak as a mortal right now," Aiden explained.

Tempest couldn't help but feel sorry for the woman who hung before her, even though she knew Soleil was responsible for so much pain and suffering.

"What are we going to do with her?" Tempest asked, her voice shaking.

"We can't kill her. That would be too easy. She needs to suffer for what she's done." Aiden's voice was hard and cold.

"But what can we do?"

"We're going to torture her. Make her feel the pain that she's caused others."

Tempest swallowed hard, her stomach-churning. She didn't know if she could handle doing something like that, even to someone as evil as Soleil.

"You don't have to do anything," Aiden said as if reading her thoughts. "I'll take care of everything. Just promise me you'll be there for me when it's over."

"No."

His head snapped towards her. "What do you mean, no?"

Tempest didn't look away from Soleil. "You can't break her, but I can. Your powers are meant for the dead. Mine are for the living."

"Tempest, the only thing you can do to her will hurt you as well. I can't let you do that."

"You and I both know she isn't the main god behind this. I won't kill her, but I need to know where Aloysius is hiding. As long as he is free, this will never end. My role among the gods is to keep them in check."

"You're sure you want to do this?"

"I never want to do this," Tempest groaned, "but I understand that I have to sometimes."

She approached Soleil and lifted the goddess's chin with her finger. "Wake up, goddess of the sun. I have some questions for you."

Soleil blinked a few times as she took in the room. She lunged at Tempest before realizing she was in chains.

Tempest pushed a small amount of her power into her voice. "*Where is Aloysius?*"

Soleil spat on Tempest's face. "If I knew, I wouldn't tell you."

Refusing to wipe it off and let Soleil see that it bothered her, Tempest continued. "*If you don't tell me, I will force it out of you.*"

"I dare you to try."

Tempest felt for Soleil's soul. She could feel the mortal souls from her trials circling the god's soul within her. While Tempest would never rip away the god's soul from their body, she wasn't afraid to take away their mortal ones and knock a god down a few levels of power.

She gripped one and ripped it from Soleil's chest.

Soleil screamed.

Tempest squeezed it in her hand and snuffed it out. "*Let's try again. Where is Aloysius? You only have so many souls left in there. How many are you willing to lose for the god of war? Do you really think he would do the same for you?*"

She could see the hesitation in Soleil's face as the goddess refused to speak.

Tempest reached out again and pulled another soul from the goddess's body.

The scream from the goddess of the sun echoed down the tunnel.

Tempest's head pounded, and she could feel her stomach turn. Her vision was already starting to swim, but she couldn't give up yet. She cleared her throat, trying to focus and pull herself back together, refusing to show any weakness.

"Please, Soleil. Tell us where he is," Aiden said.

"I can't," Soleil sobbed. "He will kill me."

Aiden's voice softened. "We will keep you here until he is contained. He will not be able to get to you."

"It won't matter. I can't do it."

Tempest raised her hand, prepared to take another soul. "*This is your last warning. Don't make me do this.*"

Soleil glared at Tempest. "You've always taken pleasure in torturing the other gods."

"*NO!*" Tempest yelled as she jabbed her finger into Soleil's chest. "*You turned me into this! I left because I couldn't take it anymore. I swear I will never let another god use me like you all did before.*"

Tempest ripped another soul from Soleil's chest and made herself step away. Her face was white, and her hands had grown unsteady.

"*I don't want to be like this, and when the balance of the land of the gods has been righted, I will happily let the gods solve their own disputes. To do that, though, Soleil, I need to know where Aloysius is so I can put a stop to this.*"

Straightening her back, she turned on her heel to face Soleil again and threw all of her power into her voice. "*SOLEIL, I COMMAND YOU TO TELL ME WHERE ALOYSIUS IS HIDING!*"

Soleil squirmed in the chains as she struggled to keep her mouth shut. Ultimately, she failed and yelled, "The land of the mortals!" She dropped into the chains holding her and sobbed harder than before.

Tempest could feel the truth in Soleil's words. She turned away to leave. "I'm sorry, Soleil. Truly, I am. I hope someday you can forgive me."

Aiden placed his hands on Tempest's shoulders as she teetered towards the wall. "You need to rest, Tempest."

She shook him off. "We need to get Aloysius before he causes more trouble."

"You are in no shape to face off with him. Rest first, fight later."

Tempest tried to argue, but her vision went black before she could come up with a response.

Tempest awoke in a soft bed. It took her a moment to remember everything that had happened before she blacked out.

She recognized the walls lined with bookshelves that surrounded her. This was Aiden's room in his palace under the mountain. Obsidian covered the arched ceiling, creating a luxurious glassy black dome above her.

Tempest rolled to her side and found Aiden bent over his desk, books and maps cluttering the surface in front of him. He looked up as Tempest stirred.

"You're awake," he said. "How are you feeling?"

"I'm fine," she said, sitting up. "How long was I out?"

"A few hours," he said. "You needed the rest."

"We need to find Aloysius," she said, swinging her legs over the side of the bed. "He could be causing all sorts of trouble by now."

"You're in no condition to face him," Aiden said. "You need to rest."

"I'm fine," she insisted. "Let's go."

Aiden walked over to the bed and sat down next to Tempest. He took her hand in his and stroked it gently. "You need to rest," he repeated. "You are not in any condition to face Aloysius."

"I'm fine," she said again. "Let's go."

"No," he said. "You need to rest. We'll set off in the morning."

He leaned over and kissed her forehead. Then he stood up and walked to the door. "I'll have someone bring you some food," he said. "Get some sleep."

Tempest lay back in the bed and sighed. Aiden was right; she was in no condition to face Aloysius. But she had to try. She had to stop him before he caused more damage.

She closed her eyes and drifted off to sleep.

Aiden walked back into the room sometime later carrying a tray of dandelion shortbread cookies and ginger tea. He placed the tray on a table next to the bed and sat down on the bed.

Tempest stirred at the sweet smell of the warm cookies. A bright smile spread across her face as she saw Aiden gesture. "You remembered."

Aiden brushed a lock of hair from Tempest's face. "How could I ever forget? You have such an odd sense of taste."

He leaned in closer, his lips inches from hers. "But that's what I love about you," he whispered.

He kissed her softly at first, but as their passion grew, their kisses became deeper and more desperate. Aiden ran his hands through her hair and down her back, pulling her closer as they kissed. Tempest ran her hands over his chest and around his waist as she returned his kisses.

Suddenly, Tempest could think of a few ways she could pass the time before morning came.

Chapter 25

The streets were eerily quiet as Tempest, Aiden, and Kirata made their way through Monstrap. It was as if the entire city was holding its breath, waiting for something to happen.

They'd left at first light, spiriting to the temple gate to travel to the land of the mortals and make their way to the emperor's palace as quickly as possible. Tempest had almost forgotten how much quicker she could travel without a mortal tagging along.

As they got closer to the city center, the streets became lined with people. They stood silently as they watched Tempest and her companions pass by.

They were blocked at the palace gates by a mob. At the head of the crowd was a man a head taller than everyone else, wearing a black hooded cloak that hid his face in shadow. As she got closer, Tempest saw that the man's eyes were glowing a bright red. If she'd had any doubt as to his identity before, it was gone now. This was Aloysius.

"What is going on here?" she demanded. "What have you done?"

Aloysius gave her a cruel smile. "I have taken control of this city," he said, "and soon, I will take control of the entire realm."

Kirata stepped forward, ax in hand, but Tempest held out her arm to stop her.

"We can't let the mortals be hurt," Tempest murmured. "You and I both know Aloysius will slaughter them without a second thought."

"You can't do this, Aloysius," Aiden announced. "The gods are not permitted to directly affect the land of the mortals."

Aloysius laughed. "Are you serious?" He pointed towards Tempest. "Tell that to the god who has lived among them for the past five hundred years! I'm sure she never had any influence on their lives."

"That's different, and you know it!" Tempest argued.

"Is it? I saw you fighting among mortals on the battlefield, choosing who would win or lose."

"Only in the wars *you* started, Aloysius. Besides, I'm not the one who has been taking possession of mortal's bodies, now, am I?"

Kirata gasped. "You've been doing *what?*"

Aloysius tossed one side of his cloak over his shoulder and drew a long sword from his side. "You're one pathetic goddess of the heavens. Really, you're all pretty pathetic. Better to replace you than put up with you."

He charged them, the air crackling around him from the chaotic energy he empowered.

Kirata stepped forward, her ax raised, and at the moment of impact, transported all of them to the middle of the desert with an ability she alone had among the gods. Spent, she dropped to her knees, panting. Aiden rushed in, sword raised, to block a crushing blow from Aloysius aimed to finish the goddess of the heavens.

"You've become weak, your majesty," Aloysius taunted.

Kirata struggled to her feet. "I've been imprisoned for a very long time and have not had time to recover fully."

Tempest summoned Soulshadow and circled behind Aloysius while he was distracted by the other two.

Kirata summoned her flagging energy, and a heavy storm cloud rolled to the middle of the battlefield over them. The cloud was so low that as the thunder crashed, it shook them to their bones. Aiden and Tempest were momentarily disoriented, but Aloysius seemed unaffected. He raised his sword and attacked.

Aiden and Tempest reacted quickly, blocking and parrying his attacks as they tried to create distance between Aloysius and Kirata. But they were quickly driven back; Aloysius was too strong, too fast. How had he managed to endure so many mortal trials and gain so many souls? Tempest wanted to reach out and strip him of them, but the effort would have finished her before it made a big enough difference.

As the battle raged on, Aiden and Tempest started to feel more and more hopeless. Their attacks were having little effect on Aloysius, who seemed intent on destroying them once and for all.

Kirata watched helplessly as the two gods were beaten back. They were no match for Aloysius. The power of the other gods was no match for the god of war head-to-head, and he seemed to have endless reserves of strength.

"We need to try something different," said Tempest, panting as she swung Soulshadow to block another blow. "There's no way we can beat him like this."

Aiden frowned, considering possible strategies in his mind. But just as he was about to speak, Aloysius whirled around them, his sword raised high in the air.

"You can't escape!" he bellowed, and brought his sword crashing down towards Aiden and Tempest, who had unwittingly been herded together.

The two gods braced themselves, knowing they would not be able to block the blow sufficiently this time. In that instant, it seemed as though all was lost.

Kirata had likewise been thinking of a way to defeat Aloysius, but she could only come up with one idea—she would have to use her own powers, despite her weakened state. Tempest and Aiden would be killed if she didn't do something. She called on the powers of the sun and the moon and directed a dazzling flash of light at the god of war's face.

Aloysius was momentarily blinded, and Aiden and Tempest took the opportunity to attack. They drove him back, but he quickly recovered and counterattacked. The three of them fought fiercely, but the gods of souls had undergone fewer mortal trials and were no match for the god of war.

He was about to deliver the killing blow to Aiden when Kirata intervened again. She called on the power of the elements and created a powerful sandstorm.

The sandy vortex appeared in the blink of an eye, and the wind surrounding them became a maelstrom of crescent-shaped dunes and swirling, mountainous blasts of wind that threatened to swallow them all up. The clouds above were darkened by sand and dirt and caked in taupe and amber, the grains falling like rain.

Kirata looked on, her face filled with concentration, her eyes burning with the intensity of the sun. The sandstorm enveloped Aloysius, and the god of war released an angry war. With a burst that blocked the sun's light, Kirata called on the storm to stop.

The gods of souls walked to where the storm had disappeared, ready to finish the job.

"Where is he?" Tempest asked.

Aloysius was gone, no trace of him left behind. Somehow, the god of war had escaped.

Kirata joined them. "We can search for his location from the land of the gods. I must return to my throne and put everything that is out of balance back in order."

Tempest and Aiden exchanged glances.

"I'm afraid we can't join you there just yet," Aiden said. "I left much unfinished in my mortal trial here."

"We'll look for Aloysius while we're here," Tempest added as she took in Kirata's crestfallen expression and the slump of her shoulders. She could well imagine how heavy the goddess of the heaven's heart was, especially considering the larger battle that was brewing. "You have our full support, Kirata. We will aid you in every way possible as we work to restore balance and order."

Aiden and Tempest returned to the emperor's palace after watching Kirata depart on her mirrored chariot. They were both covered in blood and dust from the battle with Aloysius. The guards bowed as they passed but did not say a word.

They walked through empty halls, their footsteps echoing in the silence. Most of the courtiers and servants had fled when Aloysius took over the city and the fighting started. As they approached the throne room, though, they heard raised voices inside.

"You can't just claim the throne like that! What will people say?"

"I don't care what they say."

Aiden and Tempest entered the room to find Aeon and the remaining members of the court arguing.

The courtiers' faces were drawn and tired. Some sported cuts and bruises that had been bandaged, their eyes rimmed with thick cosmetics to hide the dark circles. It was apparent the god of war hadn't taken over the city peacefully.

"Aeon will take over the throne," Aiden announced.

The room suddenly grew silent as all eyes turned towards them.

A man in emerald robes approached him. "You can't be serious."

"I am, Eb," Aiden replied. "I'm going to abdicate."

The court erupted then, each person shouting louder and louder to be heard above the others, their voices echoing down the abandoned corridors.

Aeon hurried over to Aiden. "I wasn't trying to take your spot," he explained quietly. "You disappeared with the god of war, and didn't know if you would make it back alive."

Aiden rested his hand on Aeon's shoulder and gave him a reassuring smile. "I am not offended. Besides, you are the emperor our people need right now. I am needed elsewhere."

"You are? Where?"

Tempest stepped next to Aiden. "We will hunt down the god of war."

For the second time since their arrival, the room became silent.

"I thought you had killed him and returned!" Eb exclaimed.

"When exactly did I say that?" Aiden demanded, clearly exasperated with the man. "*Never* put words in my mouth!"

"He escaped," Tempest explained.

Aiden turned back towards Aeon. "I will need your help once I find him, but in order for me to do that, I need to pass the mantle of emperor to you."

"What about the Dei Electi?" Eb interjected, then shrunk beneath Aiden's glare . "I-it was never completed. We cannot anger the gods by canceling it."

"You won't need to," Tempest smirked. "Your emperor has already chosen someone from it." She looked at Aiden, her heart full. "Technically, I think both of your emperors have."

Aiden removed his hand from Aeon's shoulder and locked his fingers with Tempest's. They gazed into each other's eyes, their hearts beating as one. They were meant to be together, and nothing could tear them apart now. They leaned close for a kiss, their lips meeting in perfect harmony.

A look of understanding crossed Aeon's face when they turned to him again, but he said nothing. Tempest studied the new emperor, wondering why someone she barely knew felt so familiar. She reached out to see his soul and suddenly understood. It was well-hidden, but she knew this soul almost as well as she knew Aiden's. She would never know how she hadn't recognized Aiden's soul earlier, but there was no doubt in her mind as to who was before her now.

Aeon was the mortal trial of Vesper, god of stars and time.

Tempest chuckled to herself.

Aloysius had no clue who he had interfered with.

Not even a god dared to challenge Fate.

The End

...for now

EPILOGUE

Aiden watched Tempest as she interacted with the young nymphs in her courtyard. They had returned to the land of the gods to make the transition of emperor less complicated. Every time he was in the room, the court deferred to him instead of Aeon—or, as Tempest had revealed, Vesper.

They told no one else of their discovery, but Aiden understood. If anyone would understand why Vesper had gone down to do a mortal trial, it would be Aiden. He had loved Tempest for centuries and would do anything to help her.

As the nymphs climbed onto Tempest, laughing and giggling, she fell over, tumbling to the ground. But Aiden just laughed along with them, enjoying the lightheartedness of this moment.

The nymphs seemed drawn to Tempest in a way that was almost inexplicable. They were enamored by her strength and beauty, admiring her from their tiny perches atop her body.

Tempest was clearly delighted by their attention, giggling as they climbed on top of her, tickling and teasing her all at once.

At last, after many laughs and moments of carefree joy, the nymphs finally dispersed back into the trees within Tempest's estate. She lay there where she had fallen on the ground amidst a collection of leaves and grass stains. Aiden gazed down at his beloved goddess with pure adoration.

"What?" Tempest asked, breathless.

"You are perfection," Aiden whispered.

Tempest smiled and closed her eyes. He knew she didn't believe it for a moment. She knew how flawed she was, but she also knew that Aiden loved her anyway.

"It's not my fault you took so long to realize how much I love you," he teased.

"Oh, I knew. Not the entire time, but I knew." She slowly stood up and brushed off her dress. "I wasn't in a place where I could reciprocate it, so I ran. It was the biggest mistake of my life, but I couldn't be who you wanted—needed—me to be then."

Aiden approached her. Brushing a stray lock of hair behind her ear, he replied, "I understand. I didn't then, but I do now, and now is all that matters."

Her grateful smile reached his soul. He pulled a small tin from behind his back and held it out in front of him.

"What's this?"

He could feel his face reddening and glanced away. "Something I made for you."

The tin disappeared from his hand, and a moment later a small squeal turned Aiden's eyes back at her.

Crumbs tumbled from her lips as she spoke with a dandelion cookie in her mouth. "You really made these?"

He swallowed, then nodded.

Her arms flew around him and she embraced him, the tin poking into his back. "You're the best thing that ever happened to me!"

"And you are the best thing that ever happened to me."

Dandelion Shortbread Cookies

1 CUP BUTTER, SOFTENED
1/2 CUP SUGAR
1/2 TO 1 CUP DANDELION PETALS (YELLOW PARTS ONLY)
2 1/2 CUPS FLOUR
1 PINCH SALT

-Separate the yellow of the dandelion flower from the stem. Careful not to green or juices or your cookies will be bitter
-Mix butter and sugar together until light and fluffy
-Add dandelion petals
-Gradually add flour and salt, Dough will be crumbly at first, but it will start to stick together.
-Roll cookies out onto floured surface and cut with cookie cutters or the top of a cup
-Bake cookies at 325 for 20 to 25 minutes, until they begin to brown on the bottoms and are fully cooked on the top.
-Allow to cool fully before eating.

Wrap Up

Thank you for reading Goddess of the Broken!

Reviews are the life blood of authors. If you have the chance, a quick review would be appreciated.

Want to get access to advanced copies of my books for free? Sign up for my Street Team to have ARC copies sent to your email.

Join my newsletter and get a free copy of The Black-Backed Mirror, a prequel to my my retelling series, and stay up to date for future releases as well as get extra freebies sent to your inbox.

You can also find me on Tik Tok @magnetra where I talk about my books and what I'm currently reading. Lol, lots of book reviews.

Behind the Scenes

Tempest demanded her story be told.

I had a cover that I made months before this book was written. This one actually. In 2022, I lost someone very close to me to mental health issues and felt broken myself. That night everything changed. The idea of a goddess who was an empath began to form in my mind. Tempest was strong, but broken. She had taken on too much from everyone around her. She mediated the other god's problems, but struggled to see those who were around her trying to help ease that burden.

This story was personal and healing for me. It became more than I had ever imagined it would be. When it began I didn't know where Tempest would take me. I just knew we would heal together.

If you struggle with mental health know that you are not alone. It may feel like it, but there are many who care. In your darkest time reach out for help. If you have nowhere else to turn, call or text the suicide hotline at 988 for those in the US.

There is absolutely NO shame in needing help.

YOU are not alone.
YOU have a place in this world.
YOU are seen.
YOU are appreciated.

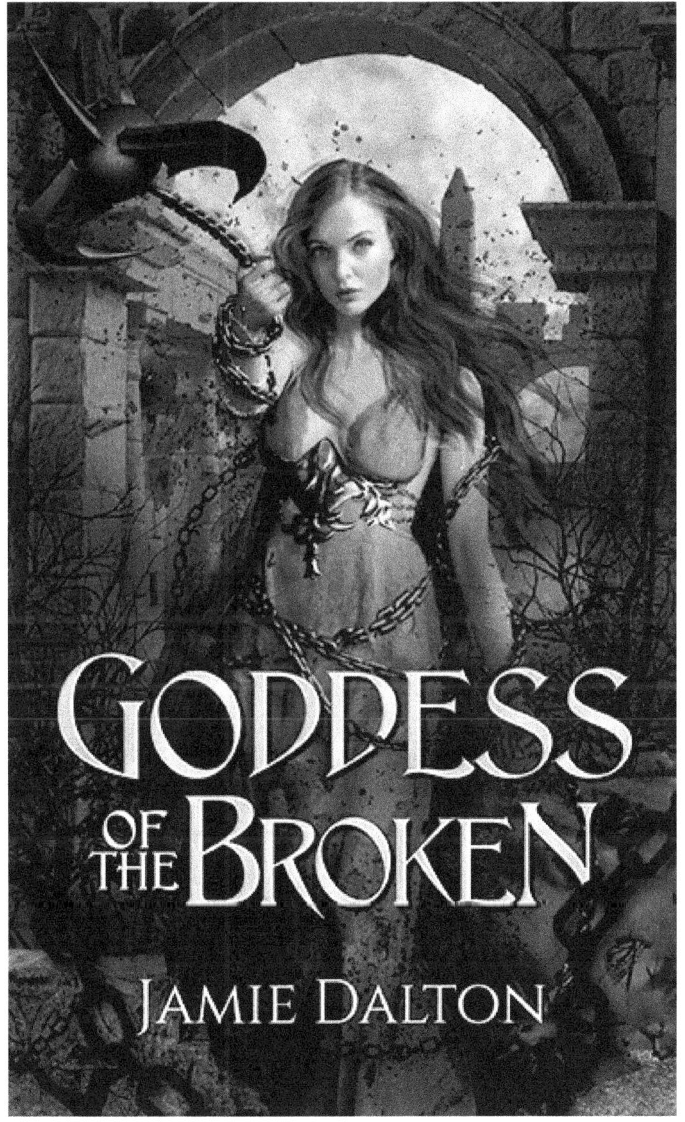
GODDESS
OF THE BROKEN
JAMIE DALTON

Thank You

First, Thank you so much to everyone who has given my books a chance. I love what I write and getting the opportunity to share these stories means the world to me.

To my beta and ARC readers, you are the best! You are what made this book go from a good one to a great one. Your encouragement helped motivate me to keep trying and add extra scenes and descriptions.

Jenny, you are amazing. The best editor and friend an author could have. I am so glad that I get to call you family and that you have been a part of this with me.

My sweet husband, Andrew, and daughter, Cassie. You both are why I do this. I know the time I spend away from you so I can write is hard and my heart misses you when I am working, but this little part of me that you allow me to share with the world means everything. Andrew, I know and see the sacrifices you make for me to do this. Financially, free time, responsibilities you are taking on... you are such a major part of why this is able to happen. I love you so much.

Trish and Alexis, you are the best! Being able to bounce my ideas off of you and share the excitement before anyone else sees it means so much. Sometimes the motivation I get from you two is why books, including this one, actually get finished.

Mom, my alpha reader. Your excitement about this book as I wrote it was a major part of what kept me going. I loved this story, but it was also hard to write. It took more out of me than I thought it would as we both healed.

My fellow Kindle Vella authors and readers, thank you!!! This book wouldn't have turned into what it did without you. Editing, the new cover, marketing... all of it came from you giving this first Vella of mine a chance and reading it. I can't believe that I am publishing a book already in the green thanks to you.

About the Author

Growing up in the mountains and forests of Oregon and Idaho, Jamie saw magic all around her. Now living in North Carolina, the fireflies and summer storms create a completely different sort of magic that inspires her just as much. Mix in the lack of sleep from raising a small child, a long list of eastern dramas with their unique tropes and the question of "I wonder what would happen if..." and you get the recipe for how these stories are created. She was a book cover designer for several years and learned the marketing side of publishing through that process so when she was ready to start putting her stories out into the world she jumped in with both feet.

www.ingramcontent.com/pod-product-compliance
Lightning Source LLC
Chambersburg PA
CBHW071337020826
48982CB00027B/1504/J

* 9 7 9 8 9 8 5 3 4 8 4 6 0 *